1022

10662

Tartton Rd

St. Louisvill

GHOSTS US
AMONGST

GHOSTS US
AMONGST

SCARY TALES FROM COLONIAL WILLIAMSBURG

Compiled by John P. Hunter

Colonial Williamsburg

The Colonial Williamsburg Foundation
Williamsburg, Virginia

Originally published in 2007 as *Witches and Ghosts, Pirates and Thieves, Murder and Mayhem: Scary Tales from Colonial Williamsburg*

25 24 23 22 21 20 19 18 17   2 3 4 5 6 7 8

Designed by Helen M. Olds
Cover design by Shanin Glenn

Library of Congress Control Number 2015051421

Colonial Williamsburg is a registered trade name of The Colonial
Williamsburg Foundation, a not-for-profit educational institution.

The Colonial Williamsburg Foundation
PO Box 1776
Williamsburg, VA 23187-1776
colonialwilliamsburg.org

Printed in the United States of America

CONTENTS

FOREWORD

G*hosts Amongst Us* is an expanded edition of a book first published in 2007 titled *Witches and Ghosts, Pirates and Thieves, Murder and Mayhem.* We have added seven new stories from Colonial Williamsburg's popular evening program "Ghosts Amongst Us."

The foreword to the first edition raised the question: Why would Colonial Williamsburg publish a book of legends, mysteries, myths, and ghost stories? It's still a valid question.

Colonial Williamsburg is as committed as we've ever been to preserving history accurately and responsibly. We operate the world's largest living history museum—the restored eighteenth-century capital of Virginia. In Colonial Williamsburg's Historic Area, you can see hundreds of restored, reconstructed, and historically furnished buildings, and you can meet the men and women who built a nation.

The stories in this book are a part of our history in that many are variations of tales told in the eighteenth century and in some cases earlier. Others are based on actual historical incidents. We have included at the end of the book notes on sources.

Colonial Williamsburg is also committed, now more than ever, to making history fun. And we hope you'll agree the stories in this book are a lot of fun.

So read on . . . if you dare!

Joseph Beatty
Manager of Historical Research
The Colonial Williamsburg Foundation

WE ARE ALL AROUND YOU

JOHN R. HAMANT

GOOD EVEN' TO YOU. Anthony Ditton at your service. I sense that you are here on a mission. You have come seeking tales of spirits and haunts and the unexplained. Nothing wrong with that. Most everyone likes a good fright. The rush of fear, the tingle up the spine, the spread of goose-flesh across their skin. Nothing but innocent fun. You know it's only a story and that you can safely retreat back into the real world once the tale is done.

When I was a boy, there was nothing I loved more than a good tale, and the more frightening the better. I would devil my father to distraction, begging him to tell me just one more. Oh, he could weave a good yarn, my father, and he knew a passel of frightful stories. He told me of ghost ships, the dead rising from their graves, witches, and the masters of the night who sucked the blood from the throats of their innocent victims.

"Tell me more, Papa, and the more horrible the better!"

The story I liked best concerned the haunted woods over in Mathews County. Father had come from there, you see, and he swore that he had witnessed all that he described.

As he told it, one night he were walking home from the store when a storm come up. He determined to leave the road and follow the shorter trail through the woods, hoping that he could arrive home before it hit. Father weren't concerned a bit. After all, he had traveled that trail scores of times, even in the dark.

He had walked through the woods a bit when he suddenly heard the clank of metal over toward the water. He stopped and listened. Another clank over to his left, and another even nearer to the right. He peered through the trees into the darkness, trying to catch sight of what was making such a curious sound.

Then he saw them. Some twenty men coming right for him. The clanking sounds filled the air, but there was no sound of their footfalls! They were no ordinary men. All was dressed in armor, and each carried a great sword. The raised visors of their helmets contained no faces but bleached white skulls with burning coals where their eyes should have been.

My father turned to flee but tripped in the tangled undergrowth and landed on his back. The dead men were on him, but they passed him by as if he weren't there, their feet walking on unseen ground an arms' length above his head! Then he saw movement far above. Gliding silently over the trees was a ship in full sail, the rotted faces of the crew peering at him over the rail.

My father enjoyed telling those tales, but little did he know that he had opened a door for me. Oh, it were hardly noticeable at first. Something gone missing, a smell, a sudden chill, or the catching sight of something out of the corner of my eye. Then I began to see them. The dead all about me. They tortured me by day and night, pressing in on me and staring, trying to touch me, all yearning to inflict pain and misery on one who still breathed. One night, overcome by drink, I lashed out at them with a knife! Come to find out I had slit the throat of a living man. I was tried and sentenced to hang.

On the day of execution I felt no fear, only hope that I would be free of the torture that had driven me to madness. There were two of us to hang that day, and two ropes had been placed on the gallows beam. I begged to go first, and the rope was placed around my neck. Before I could be turned off the cart, I jumped. Jumped to freedom! But after a few minutes, the rope broke.

I woke . . . still in hell. The sheriff removed the noose and cut my hands loose. He and the justices were arguing over whether I could be hanged twice for the same crime. Standing with them were the dead, legions of them, stretching for as far as my eye could see. And now I could smell them. Dear God, I could hear them!

Jumping up on the cart, I cursed the sheriff, telling him he weren't fit to be valet to the devil! I cursed the thousands of dead around me too, for bringing me to such an end. Placing the other noose around my neck, I jumped. This time the rope held.

Now I am with them. One of the millions of tortured souls who wander among the living. They are here with us now, but 'tis well you cannot see them. Do you feel a little tickle at your throat? A madman is slashing at it with his razor. Feel something touch your shoulder? A woman in charred clothing, her melting face dripping upon you like tallow from a candle. I warrant you are unaware of the indentured servant burying an axe into your skull as he did that of his master.

We are, in truth, all around you. Always. Watching, waiting, yearning for that door to open . . . just a crack.

Ah, the tales of spirits and haunts and the unexplained. The more horrible the better. You love them! And after all, what is the harm? It's all just innocent fun . . . or is it?

THE PALACE NURSE

ANDREA SQUIRES

THERE WAS A WOMAN WHO LIVED on a farm outside Williamsburg. She lived with her husband, Andrew, who was the stubbornest man alive. You could not talk that man out of an idea once he had it in his head. But I s'pose she was some stubborn too. Anyhow, they had lived together long and had many children, but 'twas God's will that they bury all but one. Their last living child was a lad of ten year named James. James . . . well, he was his mother's darling. He loved music. He could play the fife as well or better than anyone, and he could make up tunes too—he made up a special tune just for his ma. I reckon they was happy until everything began to change in Williamsburg.

It started with taxes. People complaining about their taxes. Soon the fools in the taverns were pounding their fists on tables and arguing about politics and saying, right out loud, that we should overthrow our king! The king whom God appointed to rule us! Can you imagine that?

Foolish talk, and Andrew drank it all in and brought it home. Night after night he read from that book *Common Sense*—the one by that Welshman Thomas Paine—until she thought her head would split. But that weren't the worst. The woman could see how little Jamie loved the talk. She could see a fire growing in Jamie's eyes, and 'twas the flame of rebellion, and of war.

She argued with the old man one night. He was in drink—alright, both were in drink—and the quarrel grew heated, until she found herself shouting at him: "Go then, you old fool, go play soldier if you've a mind! You'll be back soon enough!"

Next morning, she found he was gone. And may God rot his soul, he took Jamie with him. They needed boys to play the fifes and drums that tell soldiers what to do on the battlefield, you see.

The war came, and it lasted longer than anyone thought it would. Hard times come to everyone in Williamsburg, be they patriot or loyalist. Not that many would admit to being loyalists. The so-called Committee of Safety boys—hooligans—tormented and drove out any who dared talk against their "Glorious Cause." They even threw vegetables at the woman in the street, called her filthy names, just because she dared talk back to them. You call that liberty?

In time the woman lost the farm and took to working piecemeal when she could and begging when she could not. She was wandering one day when someone began to read out a list from the tavern steps. The list was of the dead in a battle in some heathen place up north. And on the list were the names of Andrew, and James.

The anger that took her was like a raging fire. That damnable old fool had taken from her the only thing she had left—her Jamie! She vowed that day that she would be revenged on her husband, revenged on every wretch who went about with the word "liberty" on their foul lips!

Her chance came when the Battle of Yorktown was fought. Folks in Williamsburg celebrated their great victory with feasts while she starved in the street. Her wandering took her to the Governor's Palace, now a hospital for the wounded "heroes" of Yorktown. A man come running out of the Palace and took her arm: "Missus! We need women to help nurse these men. Will you help us?"

And the spark of an idea came into her mind. "Aye," she said. "I'll help you."

For several days she mopped brows and served soup, all the while planning. Then, on a cold, clear, dry night, when everyone was asleep, she took up her lantern and she lit a pile of tinder here and a pile of rags there until the flames began to take hold.

Then she went outside and stood to watch. As the flames leapt up yellow and orange in the windows, she laughed and cried, shouting, "Burn! Burn, you traitors! Burn for my Jamie!"

And then she heard it. Music coming from an upper floor. A fife, playing a tune that only she knew.

She ran back into the blazing building, crying, "Jamie! Jamie! Where are you?" No one took notice of her as they hauled soldiers to the safety of the yard. She searched and called and the music played on until the black smoke choked her. A beam from above was falling, and that was the last thing she saw.

They say that she still walks here, condemned for her crime to search every night, lantern in hand, seeking her lost son.

Well, that's your ghost story.

Oh! I hear the tune. James? Jamie? I'm coming. It's Mama, please don't hide from me.

SAWNEY BEAN

DONNA WOLF

LONG TIME AGO, in the fifteenth or sixteenth century, in the country of Scotland, there lived a good, decent, hardworking da and mam who were cursed with a son by the name of Sawney Bean, who was by turns lazy, cunning, and vicious. When he was old enough, he ran off from his folk and met up with a woman as vicious as he was. They took up as man and wife without benefit of a church blessing.

By and by they came to the coast of Galloway and found half hidden in the rocks a cave. It was close to a mile beneath the coastline with many twisting side passages and chambers where the two foul demons could live their life as they chose. More to their style, neither man nor beast could enter the cave but twice a day, when the tide was out.

It was Sawney's plan to make their living at robbing unsuspecting travelers that rode the countryside. They would simply ambush travelers, taking from them anything and everything of value, and cut their throats to prevent them from identifying Sawney and his lady.

Some travelers were not in the habit of carrying valuables in that part of the world. This put Sawney in a bit of a quandary—no money but plenty of bodies lying about, and Sawney was not a man to waste anything of value.

By the light of a candle, man and wife dismembered and disemboweled these poor hapless folk. The limbs and edible parts were dried, salted, and pickled, then hung on hooks around the walls of the cave. A larder of human meat ready to be consumed whenever the fancy struck them. The bones were then stacked in another part of the cave, for Mrs. Bean was a most cleanly wife.

The Beans settled into their new life most readily and felt it was time to start a family. And a family it was indeed. The children learned at their father's knee to disregard their fellow man. Killing and consuming their victims was more than survival: it was a way of life for them. And the family grew to fourteen children, all of whom followed their da and mam without question. A second generation and then a third was born to carry on Sawney's legacy.

They commonly had a surplus of their abominable food, so at night they would toss legs and arms into the sea to be carried away by the tide. Bits and pieces sometimes washed up on shore all over the country. Sadly, these grisly offerings were never large enough to identify the poor owners. The authorities were at a loss for what to do, and in their mania many unfortunate arrests (and some executions) were made of people whose only crime was to be the last to see the victim before his or her disappearance.

For nigh on twenty-five years the Beans got fat and

put the fear of God into the people of Galloway. Like a pack of wild dogs, Sawney and his children were always careful to assault those weaker than themselves. Some account that, by the time they were apprehended, their victims numbered nearly a thousand. One fateful night the Beans made a mistake—their first and last.

A man and his wife traveling by one horse were coming home from a fair and fell into an ambush laid by the Beans. The man fought bravely with sword and pistol, but in the conflict his wife fell from the horse and was instantly murdered before her husband's eyes. In a thrice they had her throat cut, drinking of her blood as if it were the sweetest wine. They then ripped open her belly pulling out her entrails, readying her to be dragged off to the cave for pickling.

It was a miracle when round the bend came a group of riders numbering some twenty or thirty men also late of the fair. These brave men chased down the murdering clan, but they disappeared into the night before anyone was caught.

This sad man, the first to have ever been in the company of Sawney Bean and live to tell the tale, immediately set off for Glasgow with a hope for justice. The magistrate sent word to the king begging for his guidance.

Only three or four days later, the king himself and four hundred men set out to hunt down these devilish murderers. With the help of tracker dogs, they found the opening to the cave. Though it had no sign of habitation, the dogs set up a most hideous barking, howling, and yelping. In they went with torches held aloft. Down and down they crept venturing through the intricate turnings and windings until they beheld a most horrible sight.

It was a chamber of persons, or, more precisely, pieces

of persons: legs, arms, thighs, hands, and feet of men, women, and children hung up in rows like dried beef. And there on the floor were great masses of gold and silver, rings, swords and pistols, and large quantities of clothes, linen and woolen, thrown about in great heaps.

Sawney and his wife, their eight sons and six daughters, eighteen grandsons and fourteen granddaughters were seized and carted off to Edinburgh for sentencing. On reaching the city, the men had their arms and legs severed from their bodies and left to bleed watched by their womenfolk. The women were afterwards burned in great fires for the witches they were. At no time did the Bean family show the least sign of repentance, but died cursing with their very last breath.

But what if the king's men didn't burn all of Sawney Bean's granddaughters? What if one hid herself under the great heaps of clothes? What if she made her way to the docks and found transport to the colonies? What if she grew up and had children of her own? What if she taught those children to have the same strange appetite as their mother? What if?

REMEMBER ME

JOHN R. HAMANT

I HAVE NEED OF FINDING *SOMETHING.* Just one small spark of recognition. Just a glimmer of hope that I have not been forgotten.

Mostly my mind is hazy, in a jumble, but I do recall a cool, clear night with the stars showing brighter than I had ever seen them. In a trench with my friends. One calls out, "Moses, come give us a tune." That must be my name, for I stand and make my way toward him as I search for my mouth harp. But I am suddenly felled by a blow to the chest. A fierce blow, stronger than the kick of a horse . . . then blackness.

I remember, seems like ages before that, being on a small farmstead with a beautiful woman and two babes. I play my mouth harp, the one the beautiful woman gave me, and the babies smile and laugh while the woman sings. I kiss them all farewell and go to fight for my country, for their freedom. Endless days with too little food and too much marching. The occasional battle with them dressed in red. Crushed by the sound of cannon, muskets, and the screams of men and horses. So afraid that I will turn tail and run.

Far from home I saw a man on horseback who showed no fear. Only saw him once. Tall and stately he wore a blue uniform with bright shining buttons. We all cheered that man—our leader, our general. He had a look in his eye, a look that was fixed on something far away, something good and worthwhile and noble. I vowed to be like him. To fill my heart with hope, not fear.

Another long march, longer than I ever knew. Seems we walked for weeks, crossed a great river, and someone said we were home—back in Virginia. Days more of walking and we came to a beautiful place, a small town nestled on the bank of a great river. Then we began to dig and dig and dig. Stay to the trench, don't raise up nor stand, keep low for your life! Men die anyway. Some by shot, some by shell, but most by sickness. The smallpox cuts a wide swath.

My memories from after I was hit in the chest are very confused, just images that make no sense at all. There was a long wagon ride, me and others laid out in the wagon bed. Damned roughest ride I ever took. Heard a voice yelling, "Mind them holes! You're making these men hurt all the worse." There weren't no pain, but I did not have the strength to tell them.

It seemed like days passed by, and every time I woke I was in a room with others, all lying on straw pallets. Men and women coming and going, giving me water and some food. They would talk to me and ask me who I was, but I still lacked the strength to speak. The women would sit with me, hold my hand, and pray . . . and weep. I recall that there was an awful stink to the place, and I longed to go out into the sweet air.

One night that beautiful woman and those two babies came to me again. They kissed me, each in turn, and the woman said that she loved me. They vanished when the candles flickered. Next thing I knew I was with all these other folks. Men and women I have never seen before. More folks than I have ever seen in my life. White, Negro, Indians, and some like I've never seen before. I can't say that I know but a few of them, but somehow we are familiar to each other. Joined like brothers and sisters.

My pap used to say that the greatest treasure a man can have is to be remembered. And that makes some sense to me now. I guess the true glory of a man is what he gives to those around him, and those yet to come. Thinking back, it wasn't for myself that I went off to fight. I had nothing against them men in red, as they never did me no harm. It was for them two babies and their babies and on and on. All of us here gained our glory by giving to those yet to come. And we all keep watch, holding hope in our hearts that those yet to come will hold the blessings of freedom and liberty as close to their hearts as we did.

I will keep searching. Searching for someone who remembers me. I long for the day when I am remembered . . . by someone.

THE
WITCH OF
PUNGO

JOHN P. HUNTER

"THE MONSTER'S EYES GLOWED RED and bore into my very soul. His goat-like face and horns were scorched from the fires of hell. The hideous creature hunched and lolled his head and threatened and growled low like a hungry wolf. It was the Devil! In my house and not alone!

"Another fiend, cloaked and hooded in black, swooped at me, hovered, screeched with glee. The candlelight caught her face and I saw her clearly! It was that woman, that wicked creature . . . Grace Sherwood!

"The creature threw me to the floor with but a wave of her hand. Then she sat astride my back as if I were no more than a horse. Kicking and beating me, she forced me to carry her around my own chamber, and then we left the ground. Yes! She flogged me through the open window and up into the sky. She whipped me through the night sky and, finally, back into my house.

"My prayer book in hand, I began to back from my chamber. I cried out the Lord's name over and over, louder and louder, all the while brandishing my prayer book. In a swirl of rancid yellow smoke, they were gone.

"I fell to my knees and gave humble thanks. I also begged the good Lord to spare me any further confrontation with such malevolence, such pure evil as sits here among us . . . who sits *there* . . . Grace Sherwood! Witch! Disciple of the Devil! Witch!"

"This woman had but a dream!" screamed out Grace Sherwood as she sprang from her seat in the courtroom. "Just a dream! I am no witch!"

"Enough!" commanded the presiding judge, who just happened to be Virginia's royal governor. "Mrs. Barnes, is there anyone at all who can confirm or give credence to your testimony?"

"No, sir," she responded, "but I've spoken truthfully." She began to shake and sob under the relentless stare of Grace Sherwood. "It was no dream."

Mrs. Barnes was a witness in the trial of one Grace Sherwood, a woman accused of being a witch. The accused, a widow with three sons and a resident of the Pungo area, had been indicted by Princess Anne County Court. Now the proceedings had progressed to the General Court in Williamsburg, the highest court in Virginia, with jurisdiction over felonies for which the punishment was the loss of life or limb. The courtroom was packed.

The overwrought Mrs. Barnes was helped from the courtroom. The judge instructed the jury of gentlemen to disregard her testimony as it had no corroboration and might well have been a dream. That's as may be, but everyone knew her testimony would linger in the jurors' heads no matter what instruction they had received from His Honor.

The prosecutor, the colony's attorney general, had more

witnesses to present.

Next came Mr. Hill, a neighbor of Grace Sherwood. He recounted that a local man and Mrs. Sherwood had been in dispute over an acre of land for some time. That difference of opinion went to the local court, where the case was decided against Mrs. Sherwood. As the proceedings ended, Mrs. Sherwood made threats against her rival. After that nothing would grow on the parcel nor has anything grown on that one acre in the years since, though the surrounding acreage has no blight and is as fertile as can be. Worse yet, the man's pigs sickened the day after the trial, and all of the animals died one after another within a few days. No such malady struck any other pigs in the county.

"The man is a lazy ne'er-do-well and could not grow peas in a pod or properly raise an animal if Noah himself were his advisor!" shouted Grace Sherwood. "How is that my fault? How does that make me a witch?"

"Mrs. Sherwood!" the judge interrupted. "You are to sit quietly until properly addressed by this court. Do you understand?"

The accused clenched her jaw, nodded, and settled down, though she remained fidgety

Mr. Hill then told the court a much more horrifying tale. He and Mrs. Sherwood had had a minor argument over something trivial. The disagreement ended with a curse from the angry woman. The next morning, his wife lost the baby she had been carrying for seven months.

The attorney general called the next to testify–the grieving mother. The terrified Mrs. Hill was sworn in before God. She would not turn her face or body toward Mrs. Sherwood, who now sat like a statue.

"Mrs. Hill," the prosecutor asked, "do you have other children?"

"Oh, yes," Mrs. Hill responded, going on to say that she had no trouble carrying or birthing her three daughters. Nor had she had a moment's discomfort or a single problem with her most recent pregnancy until her husband received the threat from Mrs. Sherwood. She lost the baby the next morning.

"My innocent babe was a little boy," Mrs. Hill sobbed. "And the midwife said he was lovely and perfectly formed. There was no reason my little son should have died."

"And you? Did you experience any unusual physical suffering?"

"Never has anyone felt such pain," Mrs. Hill said through her tears. "After the baby was taken away, I lay screaming in agony. I should have preferred death to such torture."

Mrs. Hill took a few moments to compose herself as best she could, then continued in a weak voice. "For what seemed forever, but was, I'm told, only an hour or two, I lay writhing in my bed. My extremities were alternately ice cold and fiery hot. Great bolts of pain tore through my body. Muscles knotted so tightly I felt as though I was in a vice. My teeth and eyes throbbed, and my head so ached I begged my husband to end my suffering."

"I could not!" Mr. Hill shouted from the gallery.

Mrs. Hill then said that she had seen Mrs. Sherwood working in the fields wearing men's clothing.

"Have you ever tried to work all day in the fields wearing a dress?!" Mrs. Sherwood interjected loudly. "I'm just a poor widow trying to make my way!"

"One more such outburst and I'll have the sheriff restrain you," the judge said

Mrs. Hill took a deep breath and then told how her husband had briefly left her bedside to confer with the midwife about her worsening condition. "After only a minute or so and even though my eyes were filled with sweat and tears, I thought I saw a figure slip into my chamber. For just the briefest of moments, the pain subsided, and I could clearly see Mrs. Sherwood moving across the room toward my bed!"

"You are certain the woman you saw in your chamber was the accused?" asked the attorney general.

"Oh, yes!" Mrs. Hill responded. "And both my husband and the midwife saw her leave minutes later. 'Tis no doubt it was Mrs. Grace Sherwood."

"Continue, please," said the prosecutor.

"Well, sir, this witch took one more step toward my bed and the pain returned threefold. I thought surely I would die, hoped I would die rather than endure another minute of it. This evil, cursed woman began to laugh and tease me about losing my infant son. Could anything other than a witch be so cruel?

"And then?"

"My pain stopped immediately. The very instant that monster fled, my poor body's torment ended. I fear, however, that the horror and hurt she left behind in my soul might well never heal."

Mrs. Sherwood sat unblinking throughout Mrs. Hill's testimony but now screamed out, "I went to offer a neighbor my heartfelt sorrow over her baby's death! That is all I did! The rest is hallucination!"

The presiding judge then asked Mrs. Sherwood if she had any questions for Mrs. Hill. She replied that she had no interest in hearing more of a deranged woman's delusions. "Every word from this woman's mouth is nothing more than recounting the nightmare she must have experienced. Why she includes me in the telling is a mystery. Get her away from me."

With that, Mrs. Hill was excused. The attorney general of the colony of Virginia once again took the floor to sum up the proceedings and his case against Grace Sherwood. He explained that charges involving witchcraft in one form or another passed through his office from time to time. Until the Sherwood case, however, he had never once chosen to prosecute one. The records sent his office by Princess Anne County officials were so compelling that he saw no alternative but to bring the case to trial in the General Court. Princess Anne officials performed the accepted tests for witchcraft properly and the results were most disturbing if not damning. For example, it was a well-known fact that witches' bodies were marked by the Devil. The marks were generally dark in color and easily distinguished from birthmarks, scars, moles, or other common skin discoloration as they were odd in shape, had no feeling, and did not bleed.

"Our distinguished colleagues in Princess Anne County carried out this test on Mrs. Sherwood in a public, legal, and well-documented manner," the attorney general said.

A panel of twelve matrons of respectable reputation was assembled to examine the body of the accused for the telltale spots. Between them, they had assisted many women in the births of their children. The female anatomy was no mystery to them. When they inspected Mrs. Sherwood's body, they discovered some very strange dark, almost black, marks on her lower torso.

"I have here the sworn deposition of these twelve, properly witnessed and executed. They are all in complete agreement that, upon seeing these marks, they pricked them with needles, but Mrs. Sherwood felt nothing, and the marks did not bleed," the attorney general said as he presented the deposition.

"What have you to say, Mrs. Sherwood?" the judge asked.

"Your honor," she said, "I was born with those marks. They have always been on my body and were certainly not administered to me by the Devil or anyone else. They are just marks, sir. I've had them all my life."

"Is there anyone . . . a kinswoman, neighbor, midwife . . . who could swear that you have had these marks since you were an infant?"

"I . . . no, sir," Mrs. Sherwood said. "No one."

The attorney general described a second test that was, he assured one and all, also carried out in a perfectly legal way and witnessed by Princess Anne County gentlemen of unquestioned character and honor. The test was a trial by water. Water was a pure element and witches most certainly were not. Therefore, water would reject a true witch. The accused was bound hand and foot and dropped into water over her head. If she sank and drowned, embraced by the water, she was not a witch. If she floated and escaped drowning, rejected by the water, she was a witch.

"On the appointed day, Grace Sherwood was accompanied by many witnesses including the aforementioned gentlemen to a river in Princess Anne County. She was then bound hand and foot. Gentlemen, it was not a task to be taken lightly. The knowledge that a woman so bound was to be cast into water over her head weighed heavily on the attending men. Why, no righteous man of good heart takes pleasure in a duty such as this. Our human compassion for our fellow creatures rebels at such an action. And, yet, they knew their duty. If there was a witch in their fine county, they needed proof, so the trial by water provided a crucial piece of evidence."

Accordingly, Grace Sherwood was dropped into the river. Everyone in attendance craned forward, some full of hope, some with dread.

"A most unprecedented thing then occurred," the attorney general. "Mrs. Sherwood not only did not sink beneath the water, she floated *above* it!"

Astonished exclamations rang out in the courtroom. The judge held up his hand for silence. He let out a long sigh before asking, "Mrs. Grace Sherwood . . . can you explain to this court what happened? Have you any explanation at all?"

"I have the good Lord to thank!" Mrs. Sherwood. "I prayed to the gracious Lord to save me, spare me, not let me drown, and he answered my prayers! God saved me! That is my explanation."

"I see," said the judge.

"Members of the jury and gentlemen of the court," the attorney general continued in a somber tone, "I am bound by law and duty to prosecute cases to the best of my ability. In some trials, the facts of the case are open to interpretation, the witnesses vague, and circumstances murky. However, in the case of Mrs. Grace Sherwood, brought up on witchcraft charges, even if you set aside witness accounts of visitation by fiends, there are still the results of the tests laid out by the law to determine if one is a witch. If that person fails the tests, as did Mrs. Sherwood, that person is then, by definition, a witch and must be convicted and sentenced as such."

A hush fell over the courtroom. After almost two minutes of silence, the judge asked the prosecutor, "Is there not one more test that is sometimes rendered in these cases?"

"Yes, your honor," came the reply, "although it does not carry the same weight as the others, there is, indeed, one more test. It is said that a witch cannot recite the Lord's Prayer."

The judge nodded, exhaled and asked, "Mrs. Sherwood, can you recite the Lord's Prayer?"

"Oh, yes, your honor! Yes, indeed!"

"I certainly hope so," responded the judge. "Proceed."

Everyone in the courtroom leaned forward.

"Oh, heavenly Father, uh . . . hallowed be . . . kingdom comes, um . . . on earth as . . . ," she stuttered. It got worse. Each attempt was only a few words or scattered phrases before she fell apart and shook with the struggle.

At last, Mrs. Sherwood gave up and began to sob uncontrollably. "I know the prayer well," she wailed. "There are so many eyes and ears on me! I am not a witch! I am not a witch!"

The judge rubbed at his temples and then said, "Do you have anything else to add, Mrs. Sherwood?"

"I am no witch!" she cried. "These people spew forth these untruths to cover their own failings! They need someone to blame for their shortcomings. It is all untruth! I am but a hardworking widow and mother!"

After a moment, the judge said in almost a whisper, "This court will now poll the gentlemen of the jury and render its verdict."

"Those say guilty, so indicate," said the clerk in a loud voice. He carefully counted the raised hands.

"Those say not guilty, so indicate," the clerk said as he moved down the aisle. As carefully, he counted the raised hands. After he recorded the numbers in a small book, he turned to the judge and said, "We have a verdict, your honor."

What was it? What was Grace Sherwood's fate?

* * * * *

In later years, court records of the proceeding were

moved to Richmond for safekeeping, only to be destroyed in a fire in the nineteenth century. Some say Mrs. Sherwood served seven years in prison and then returned home to her land and children, but imprisonment was not routinely used as a punishment in colonial times. Still others say she was acquitted. No one knows for sure.

The only thing that is certain is that Mrs. Sherwood lived another forty years after her trial for witchcraft. A last will and testament for a Mrs. Grace Sherwood is proof of that.

HITCHHIKING SPIRIT

PATTI VATICANO

THERE ONCE WAS A SIMPLE FARMER and his wife, plain and decent folk for the most part, though the wife was uncommonly superstitious. She believed in all manner of omens and spells and maintained that evil spirits were always out and about waiting to do mischief to the unsuspecting. They say she had shoes buried beneath every hearthstone in her house and witch balls hung at every window, both means of trapping conjuring spirits. She meant well, of course, but her husband had precious little patience with all her wails and warnings. The farmer was stiff-necked, prideful, and not inclined to bow his head to flesh nor spirit. He had all he could do to keep his wife's fears and superstitions from driving him to distraction.

One morning, the farmer was preparing to drive into town to trade, but the wife would have none of it. She claimed that several omens of death had come to her over the days preceding and begged him to put off the journey. She insisted she'd heard a rooster crowing after dark in the early part of the week and had heard, not once, but twice, their old hound howling and whining at nothing while staring at the ground. And hadn't the farmer himself missed a row of corn while planting the north field on Tuesday? She insisted that all of these occurrences were signs of death and the farmer had best put off trading for another week.

"Death won't be denied a companion, once he's made the trip," the wife pleaded. The farmer dismissed her fears and drove his loaded wagon down the one road that led in to town.

Town trading went better than usual for the farmer that day, and by the time he'd readied the wagon for the return home, the sun was low in the west. Only a few miles into his journey, he was traveling the lonely road in the light of a full and early-rising moon. He wasn't at all fearful of either the hour or the way. The road was washed in a soft silver light, and every bush and tree limb was as clearly defined as though the noonday sun were shining.

After he'd taken a familiar bend in the road, the farmer saw a lone figure. It was peculiar, a man by himself out at such an hour in a desolate area with no horse, but there he stood. There was no mistaking it for a trick of the eye or the moonlight as the man was clearly motioning to the farmer to draw up the wagon.

The farmer was thinking on the curiosity of the situation when, without warning, his horse took off at a dead run, giving the stranger a wide berth as it ran past. The farmer struggled mightily to control the horse and wagon. When the animal finally slowed down, the farmer found himself nearly a mile from the spot where the stranger stood. He continued on toward home, not being inclined to turn back.

The farmer traveled on for another half hour with little

thought in his head save for the supper waiting for him at journey's end. Then . . . could his eyes or the hour be deceiving him? He saw what looked like the same stranger standing off to the side of the road, miles from the place where the farmer first saw and passed him! It couldn't be, the farmer thought, must be another man. Still, the farmer was disturbed by the notion that, unaccountably, it certainly *looked* like the same man. He had little time to think on it. Once again, as he neared the stranger, his old horse broke into a mad dash and the wagon had gone nearly a mile before the farmer could rein him in.

The farmer labored over the oddity for a good while, turning it over every way possible in his mind as they continued on down the road. Just when the farmer had convinced himself that it wasn't the same man, that it must have been a coincidence or maybe the moonlight, there was what looked like the very same form standing by the side of the road for a third time! Now the farmer was spooked, and his wife's words came back to him: "Death won't be denied a companion, once he's made the trip." And that did it. The farmer didn't wait for the horse this time. He set the animal at a run so fast that the planks of the wagon creaked and groaned, threatening to break apart. In a flash, they were past the figure and a good distance beyond. As they galloped past the man, the farmer felt the stranger's gaze and shuddered.

By the time his nerves had settled, the farmer was almost home and silently congratulating himself for outwitting fate. He began wondering if there would be corn hoe cakes for supper. Then he heard the slow and mournful sound of the old wagon boards creaking as though a groaning weight had been laid upon them. He turned and saw, to his horror, sitting at the far end of the wagon, the very figure he'd passed three times! It sat there calm and peaceful with a pallid face grinning wide at him in the bright moonlight!

This was too much for any man! The harried farmer thought of jumping clear of the wagon and running, but his pride would not let him. He was determined to outdistance Death—for surely, his passenger could be none other—and be home and safe by his fireside within the hour. Using all the power of his legs, the farmer gave one mighty thrust and leaped onto the back of his horse. The brave man intended to cut the horse free of the rolling wagon and ride him away from the danger. It was a sound idea, but just as he reached back to cut the traces, the terrified horse reared up in its harness!

The farmer was thrown backward and down. He was suspended between the horse and wagon, caught up in the mass of tangled and twisting traces and totally helpless to right himself. With every attempt to do so, he only dropped lower and lower until he was being dragged along the ground by the crazed animal and careening wheels of the driverless wagon. In the end, the farmer was dragged to the very threshold of his homestead where his good wife found him. He was nothing but a mangled, bloodied, and lifeless corpse.

And there you have it. No one can outdistance Death— *for he simply won't be denied a companion, once he's made the trip.*

BROKEN HEART

RUTH TSCHAN

OVER YONDER ACROSS THE RIVER in Gloucester County stands an old, old house. 'Twas built, it remember me, around about the year of our Lord sixteen hundred and fifty. It stands in the shadow of a grove of old oak trees. To the back the gardens are terraced down to the shore of the beautiful Ware River.

For many a year this old house has been shrouded in mystery and sorrow; however, the old walls hold memories of happier times, of banquets and balls, good company, good conversation. Visitors will tell you that, to this day, if you listen sharp in the still of the night, you can still hear the sound of laughter through the house and the rustle of a lady's silk skirts as she moves through the passageway and up the staircase.

So many generations have come and gone, would it not be strange if no ghosts ever walked those silent halls? But, watch as you may, you will never catch even a fleeting glimpse of a diaphanous white-shrouded wraith moving about. Nor hear nary a creak or moan that cannot be accounted for. You know, most of the noises heard in old houses can be explained away—an old house settling into the storm creaks and the wind wuthering through the eaves sounds for all the world like the moaning and groaning of a long lost soul. Except on one night of the year—the night of the first snowstorm of the winter.

It happens on this wise . . .

The family will be sitting quietly reading or chatting, and then a hush falls over the room, and they listen. You can hear a log being thrown on a ghostly fire in the chamber overhead and hear the crackle of the fire as the tinder catches and burns. Someone in the family will move to the window and, drawing aside the curtain, say, "Oh, it's beginning to snow." And they know that, with the coming of the first snow, the spirit of a long-dead, beloved daughter of the family has come back once more to hearth and home. Perhaps she is seeking the warmth and love of family. Though this gentle daughter makes her presence felt but once a year, always she is greeted with love and sympathy, never with any dread.

The name of this ghostly maiden has been lost in the mists of time. Some say as how it were Elizabeth. Methinks we just don't know. We do know she were a Throckmorton. Her papa was a man of considerable means. Methinks she were ever so little bit spoiled. Never knew a papa yet—including my very own, God rest his soul—who didn't delight in spoiling a daughter. Mr. Throckmorton was no exception. He loved to buy beautiful silks and satins right off the boat from England for her and priceless jewels from the Orient and from all over the world.

Most any pretty day you might see her walking through the gardens, hear the rustle of her silks, and see the sparkling of her beautiful jewels. And her face—it was a happy face. A young man had come along and quite stolen her heart away. She was young and beautiful and in love. She had most everything to make a young lady happy. Except for one thing—her papa's approval. That young man in no way pleased her papa. He said, "No. No, Daughter! All he's after is your money. You send him away and tell him you never want to see him again." She was a most obedient and dutiful daughter. She yielded to his wishes. She sent the young man away and she never saw him again. But she kept her love for him in her heart and grieved for the loss of him. She pined away, and after a while this lovely blossom of a girl faded away and gave up the ghost.

On a cold, blustery day in November the grieving father had to take this beautiful child to the old family burying ground in the garden on the hilltop overlooking the old Ware River and lay her to rest in a grave there. Stricken with remorse, in one last loving gesture, he decided to have her buried with her jewels still on.

As Mr. Throckmorton made his way back to the house through the dead garden, he was so wrapped in his sorrow he was unaware of the falling of the night shadows and the rising fury of the storm. The snow had begun to fall, the first snow of the season, snow upon snow. He went into the house and threw himself into the great chair beside the hearth, unaware even of the passage of time.

Huddled forlornly by his fire, his heart heavy with grief, he finally realized that the room had grown chill and the embers were burning low. He dragged himself up to fetch another log for the fire. He stopped in mid-step, cocked his head to listen. Had he heard something? What was it he had heard? It sounded like a scratching at the door. Naw, he thought, 'twas naught but the scratching of a branch against the windowpane or one of the dogs seeking shelter from the cold. He paid it no more mind. He never went to the door. He fell again into his chair and sat far into the night, never really sure when the scratching had ceased. Morning found him still sitting, now by the cold, dead embers on the hearth.

A slave came 'round to see if he mightn't want some breakfast and to air out the room, rid it of the smells of old ashes and smoke from the night before. He threw open the door on the garden slide of the house. At his feet lay a heap of drifted snow upon the doorsill. Dusting it aside with the toe of his boot, he was horrified—it 'tweren't no dog under the snow, it was the cold, stiff, dead body of the master's daughter. As her father once again gathered her into his arms he saw the pool of blood that lay all about her.

Now you may well ask, how in the world did she get from the burying ground to the house in the middle of the night?

It were on this wise . . .

Two of the Throckmorton slaves knew she was to be buried with her jewels on, and they had determined to rob the grave. They had gone in the dead of night, scraped away the fresh-laid earth, opened the coffin, and attempted to remove the priceless rings from her cold fingers. The rings just would not come off, no matter how hard they tried. So in his haste and in his greed, one of the slaves whipped out his hunting knife and cut her fingers clean away!

From the time I were a tot I have been in mortal dread of being buried alive. So she had been. Now the doctors tell us that there is a sort of fainting sickness—they call it a coma. 'Tis for all the world like death itself and folks is buried. So she were. They also tell us that if in some manner the blood can be got to flow again, sometimes these folks can be resurrected, brought right back from the dead. That's so! So she were. The blood began to flow and she began to stir. Need I tell you more about those two slaves? Never saw hide nor hair of them again, nor the jewels neither.

Somehow, even with her poor mangled hand, she were able to drag herself out of that grave and claw her way through the snow, her shroud dragging through the dead stalks of the garden, crawling and stumbling until she reached the haven of home. She fell upon the doorstep, and all strength failed her. She was barely able to scratch upon the door. Any cry she may have made was whipped away on the howling winds. She could hear her father moving about inside, replenishing his fire. He never went to the door. Slowly she was shrouded once more, this time beneath the falling snow—snow upon snow.

And so it were that the grieving father once more had to take his beloved daughter to the empty, waiting grave in the old burying ground on the top of the hill. But, every year, on the night of the first snow of the season, she returns, coming back to hearth and home, seeking warmth and love and family . . . and, always, always she is welcomed with love and sympathy.

This is a very sad tale, but I would like to leave just one more thought with you. As you move about this old city—and it is a very old city—there are many wandering souls about. Oh, they are there, you just take my word for that. You may find yourself encountering some of these spirits. Should you have such an encounter, here or at home or wherever you may go, please greet them with love and sympathy, never any dread.

DARK
CORNERS

PATTI VATICANO

DO YOU BELIEVE IN THE WORLD UNSEEN? I'm not talking about ghosts, now. Ghosts are harmless creatures for the most part. Lost and confused most often, I say. Timid-like, and similar to ourselves. Ghosts were once human beings, weren't they? No, I'm not talking about ghosts. I'm talking about things, things that may never have been human. Agents of a greater evil than you or I could ever imagine! Things that wait to do us harm—to steal our very souls. I never gave such things a moment's thought until I crossed paths with Moses Riggs.

Moses Riggs is an old man who walks the streets of Williamsburg here in the evening, just as the sun is setting. He wanders about aimlessly, almost like a ghost himself, sometimes in and among the trees of the Commons, other times along the graveyard wall of Bruton Church. Although people here in Williamsburg say Moses Riggs is insane, I say we little know what insight may be given those people you and I call mad.

Close to seven years ago, just north of here in Accomack County, Moses Riggs did a hideous thing. Early one morning, he murdered a poor, young Negro boy, coldly and without conscience or heart. The young boy's name was Stepney, and he was a slave, the property of a Mr. Benjamin West of that same county. The murder was a ghastly act, just ghastly.

Early that morning, with the heavy stock of an old gun, Moses Riggs dashed the brains out of that poor, young Negro boy. Then, with the muzzle of the gun, he punctured that poor boy's body so as to, he claimed, let the green poison drain out. Moses was found later that day with blood and brains all over him and the muzzle of the gun. When the authorities arrested him and asked how he could commit such a foulness, he answered calmly and with a leveled gaze, "Well, I killed the Devil, and that's all there is to be done about it."

Moses claimed that just as the moon and stars were winking out that morning, he saw a small demon enter into the boy's body and that the same would have enacted great, malicious mischief all about the county if he, Moses Riggs, had not done just as he did. He added that when the boy was dead and the body still, he saw, in his words, the wretched little Satan free itself from the boy's body and go flying off into the wind, howling and shrieking as it flew. I had the sad occasion, thereafter, of seeing that poor boy's body.

Moses was brought here to Williamsburg and, after court proceedings, housed in the public gaol. They kept him there almost six years while trying to decide whether he was a murderer or a madman. In the end, they let him go. I've never been sure of the reasons. Perhaps it was because they believed the years had, at last, burned the madness out of him or, perhaps, because they believed that all but Negroes were safe from his hand.

It was myself who brought Moses his food those six years, and I can tell you this: Moses Riggs is a strange man. He's always talking about haunts and apparitions and the world unseen, and he has strange and peculiar beliefs too. The strangest of which, the one people find hardest to believe, is that demons and all manner of foul and unholy creatures lurk in corners, any corners they can find, but most especially dark, sharp, angled corners. From such places, they are always watching us, always waiting, always listening so they may enter into our world to do us the most grievous harm of body and of soul.

Moses is always staring off into corners and giving such places wide berth. He never takes shelter indoors, except in churches, despite the most severe of weathers. He declines the most charitable of invitations. He never lingers long in either public or private dwellings. Even his home, if you can call it such, is a hollowed out old oak tree, as large and round as a gristing stone! It's the only place he'll rest, you see, for it's the only place that's free of corners and sharp angles.

Though I rue it now, I came to know Moses very well those six years he was housed in the public gaol, most especially once he had been brought inside to the inner cells where they housed the insane.

He was no trouble. Truly! He was no trouble at all except for the talking. Oh, the incessant talking! Sometimes for hours at a time to no one in particular in his cell, sometimes in his own voice and sometimes, as I thought then, in a voice feigned or pretended.

Weeks, then months, then years went by like that for poor Moses with little change, and I were there for much of them. Then it happened! I had come, as was my custom, with his evening meal, but as I approached the cell this time, this time I heard two voices, two distinct voices, speaking at once and in an agitated manner! They were having an argument in there! I thought, at first, that a visitor had come but was just as quick to realize that no visitors would have been allowed in so late in the evening, nor would they have had such familiarity with Moses Riggs had they come. I heard the voice that did not belong to Moses punctuate his words with a low and venomous hissing sound. I tell you, it chilled me to the very marrow to hear it! But I was curious and lowered myself down slowly to peer into the cell through the food slot in the door.

I could see little at first due to the lateness of the hour and the dimness of the cell, little but the outline of Moses himself, his rolled-up sleeping pallet, and the remnants of his previous meal. Then my eyes grew more accustomed to the darkness, and I could see more plainly. There, in the left-hand corner of the cell, across from where Moses sat in *a dark, sharp, angled corner*—and it was no play of shadows, I tell you!—there in that corner I saw the most horrific and malevolent form. It was not human and yet, somehow, it was human-like. It was torturously shaped, grotesquely deformed. It was small and black, and yet I could sense a great and oppressive depravity coming from that corner and such a wicked intent.

I screamed, and, at my outcry, the shape of the creature disappeared, but the shape only. *Not its eyes.* Its eyes remained in that corner, hovering there, disjointed from its body, yellowed and jaundiced and filled with hate. God have pity on me! Those eyes! They leveled upon me and held me fast! They searched my soul through and through! It recognized me, don't you see? God have mercy on me! It recognized me!—and tried to lay claim to my very soul!

I little know what happened next. They say I was in a long delirium for weeks and that there was talk of committing me to the public hospital here in Williamsburg as a lunatic. I have no recollection of it, no recollection of it at all. But they tell me good people came and prayed over me. Day and night they prayed over me and in the end, I was saved from the darkness, spared those shadows that had long ago claimed poor Moses Riggs. And now, it is only in prayer that I feel safe.

Once, thereafter, I came upon poor Moses in his wanderings. I have no words to tell you the horror and fear that rose up in me when I saw him. But our eyes met, and we communicated, each to the other, a sad and terrifying knowledge of our world that I wish we did not have. I wish I did not have it now!

Listen to what I tell you: beware dark corners and where sharp angles meet, for they are always waiting for us there. Always watching, always listening, always waiting for us there.

TURNING SKULL

JONATHAN HALLMAN

IT SETS SOME FOLK ON EDGE TO LEARN that there's a graveyard right here in the middle of town. 'Course, there ain't no point in bein' superstitious 'bout graveyards cause all they is is full of dead people. And you know what dead people does, don't ya? Lies around! That's all. Ain't nothin' to be scared of when it comes to all them dead folk lyin' around in graveyards.

On the other hand, all them poor dead folks has plenty to be worried about from us walkin' around on top of the earth. See, there's always someone lookin' to dig 'em up. Where do you think the apothecaries get the bodies they use to study anatomy? That's right! They get 'em from graveyards. Not that they dig 'em up themselves, mind you. They leave that work to the folk they calls resurrection men. They's called that 'cause their job is raisin' the dead. Mostly in the middle of the night, mind you—it ain't strictly legal. But they goes out and digs up them dead bodies and sells 'em, to apothecaries and surgeons and such.

But they ain't the only ones diggin' up them poor dead

folks and puttin' 'em through all sorts of troubles! In fact, I just heard a story a short while ago about just such a thing. Mind you the tale come from France, and you know them Frenchies is some strange people, but it proves the point.

You see, in this little village over there in France, there was a couple of grave diggers, and they'd been called upon by the family of a fellow who'd just passed on—I believe his name was Mr. Rich. Anyway, his kinfolk naturally wanted a place dug for Mr. Rich to rest. So them grave diggers took up their shovels and made their way out of town to the graveyard and set about findin' a suitable spot to dig a grave for Mr. Rich.

All the grave diggers I've ever spoken to says that the best place to dig a grave is one where there ain't no headstone. So they found themselves such a spot there in the graveyard and set about diggin'. And diggin'. And diggin'. You see, it's a lot of diggin', 'cause them graves is deeper than I am tall! But anyway, while they was diggin', they struck something and it sounded like wood. Now, that made them a bit nervous, you see, and when they cleared away the dirt to see what they had struck, well, it proved to be the lid of a coffin that weren't supposed to be there! They'd chosen a spot without a headstone for that very reason and now here someone was, lyin' in the grave that they was diggin' for Mr. Rich!

They found themselves in a bit of a quandary, 'cause they wasn't sure who the grave should belong to. On the one hand, they'd heard said that possession is nine-tenths of the law, and the person lyin' there in the grave could be said to be in possession of it. If that was the case, the grave should belong to him. On the other hand, if it was the family of Mr. Rich who was payin' for the grave, didn't that mean whoever was lyin' in it was trespassin' on their property? And that bein' the case, oughtn't the trespasser be removed in favor of the payin' tenant?

Like I says, they was quite puzzled, but after thinkin' about it for a bit, they decided that whoever was payin' won. So they took up their shovels, broke through the lid of the coffin, and set about removin' the trespasser. First a leg bone . . . then another leg bone . . . then arm bones and rib bones. There's lots of bones in a body, you see. At last, one of them reached down and picked up the skull and set it up alongside the grave. Then they took up their shovels and went back to diggin' to make sure they'd got rid of the rest of the coffin, that the grave was deep enough, and all that.

Now, while they was diggin', one of them fellows thought that, out of the corner of his eye, he could see somethin' movin' up by the edge of the grave. So he set down his shovel and turned to see what it was. He could swear that he saw that skull turn and look right at him. He elbowed his partner in the side. That second fellow turned to see what he was bein' beaten upon for. The first fellow didn't say nothin', he just pointed. So the second fellow set down his shovel and looked up and, sure enough, that skull turned and looked right at him too! The two of them fellows jumped so high they cleared the side of that grave by a good couple of feet and hit the ground runnin'.

They headed back to the village as fast as they could and set about lookin' for the wisest person they could think of 'cause they was convinced by now that that skeleton they'd dug up was possessed by the Devil. It prob'ly wanted to take their souls! Of course, it bein' a French village, the wisest person they could think of was the priest.

They run through the church doors, found the priest, and told him all about what had happened there in the graveyard. The priest just looked at them grave diggers like they was a couple of lunatics. After all, who ever heard of a skull turnin' back and forth and lookin' at people?

They did tell him all about what had happened in the graveyard includin' how they'd decided who the grave should belong to. The priest wasn't at all happy about that, and the more he thought about it, the more upset he became. He decided he ought to investigate the matter in person. So, when he got them grave diggers settled down, he had them lead him out of town to the graveyard to show him where they'd been diggin'.

When they come to the edge of the graveyard, them grave diggers refused to go a step further. No matter what that priest told 'em, they was still convinced that that skeleton was possessed by the Devil and they wasn't goin' no closer to it than they had to. So, they just pointed off toward where they'd been diggin' and sent the priest on his way alone.

The priest made his way on through the graveyard. As he come toward where they'd been diggin', he saw the grave, and them bones, and that skull, which was just settin' there starin' into the grave. When that priest come within about ten paces of that grave, the skull started to turn! It turned all the way around and set them empty eye sockets right on that priest.

"Alleluia!" shouted the priest. "It's a saint!" France is full of saints, after all. They got all sorts of 'em. They got St. Isidore, and St. Bernard, and St. Louis, St. Denis . . . I don't know what all.

Anyhow, that skull lyin' there on the ground . . . well, the priest didn't know who this new saint was 'cause there weren't no headstone there to tell him, but he was sure it was a saint. He called them grave diggers over from the edge of the graveyard and gave them instructions to go back to the church. They was to fetch a fine silvery tray and some fine white linen cloths and set someone to ringin' the church bell to call all the villagers to gather together.

They was gonna' have a mass to celebrate this new saint. Meantime, the priest, he was gonna' stay there in the graveyard and make sure nothin' happened to the saint. I think he was hopin' the saint might speak to him, but it didn't. The priest and the saint, they just set there lookin' at each other 'til them grave diggers returned with the tray and them cloths.

Then, the priest took the tray and set it down there on the ground by the saint. Then he took one of them fine white linen cloths and laid it on the tray. Very carefully, he bent down, said a prayer, and picked up that saint's skull and set it there on the tray. Then he picked up the rest of them bones and spread them on the tray as well. He spread another one of them linen cloths over the top of it all and then led them grave diggers back into the village.

Now in the meantime, the ringin' of the church bell had brought all them villagers to their doorways to see what was goin' on. They saw this little procession headed toward the church so they just naturally joined in. By the time they got to the church doors, it was a grand parade. Everyone in the village was there. The priest, he led 'em in and made his way on up to the altar. All the rest of 'em just naturally filed into the pews. The priest set that tray up on the altar, said a prayer, and then folded back that fine white linen cloth, revealin' them bones . . . the skull front and center. Then he made his way over to the pulpit to say the mass.

All them folks out in the pews was all excited. They was whisperin' to each other and pointin' and whisperin' and pointin'. The priest, he just waited for 'em all to settle down, but they wouldn't stop! They just kept on pointin' and whisperin'! At last, the priest turned to see what they was all pointin' at and whisperin' about and there, on the altar, that saint's skull was turnin'!

Back and forth it turned, as if lookin' out through them empty eye sockets at everyone in the congregation. Then that saint's skull, it stopped turnin' and focused its gaze on them open church doors out there at the end of the aisle. Everyone fell silent 'cause that saint's skull, it started to open its mouth! To speak! And everyone waited to see what the saint would say.

Just then, a little furry brown mole popped out of that saint's mouth, jumped down off the altar, and ran down the aisle and out them doors! And that was the last anyone ever saw of that saint!

Maybe that's why the French have so many saints. Easy come, easy go!

THE TELLTALE FINGER

MELANIE COLLINS

A YOUNG LADY WAS VISITING HER grandparents on their farm. Late one afternoon, the girl and her grandfather were sitting in front of the house discussing important matters when a tall man wearing a long black coat and clutching a bible walked out of the woods. Except for his great height, the man did not seem dangerous, but the girl's grandfather sent her inside just to be on the safe side.

"What business have you?" the grandfather asked.

"Only the Lord's business, sir," the tall man replied. "I am but a simple preacher in hopes of finding a place to rest my weary head for the night."

Wary of strangers, the grandfather said, "Perhaps you are a man of the cloth, perhaps not. I have women here to protect, and I'll not be putting them at any risk. You may not pass the night under my roof."

The tall man answered. "Perhaps a barn? I truly do not think I can walk another mile this day."

The grandfather thought a minute and then said, "There's an abandoned house cross the field there. Not much it is, but you may lodge there if you please."

The preacher cleaned out a space for himself in the old, falling down house. By nightfall, he had a fire going in the fireplace and was sitting in a lopsided rocking chair enjoying a biscuit and dried meat. Content, he moved closer to the light of the fire and began reading his bible. He'd read no more than one page when he heard a rooster crowing at the front door. A rooster crowing after dark could only be a bad omen. But the preacher, being a man of God, did not believe in such superstitions and continued to read his bible. After an hour or so, he dozed off.

He was jolted from sleep by a low moaning sound. He woke to see the wispy, white figure of a young woman hovering in the air. She was wrapped in a flowing white cloth, and her big eyes were tortured and full of tears. The preacher clasped his bible to his chest with fear, but before he could say a prayer, the ghostly woman wailed in a deep hollow voice, "Heeeelp meeee. Please put me to rest."

The preacher wanted to run or fall down to his knees and pray for protection, but he was frozen to his chair. He could now see the woman more clearly. She was young, perhaps twenty-two or twenty-three. Her hair was hanging loose and ragged about her shoulders, her clothes were torn and dirty. She might have been pretty once, he thought, but now, where her eyes had once been were two gaping black holes. She spoke in a hollow voice.

"I was murdered in this very room. My bones lie beneath that hearth. Heeeelp meeee."

The preacher gathered up all of his faith and strength and asked, "Wha . . . wha . . . what do you want from me?"

"You must dig up my bones," she said. "Break off the little finger of my left hand and pass it among all twelve neighbors in the countryside. The finger will identify my murderer."

The preacher was shaking and held his bible even tighter.

"Only then can I rest in peace. Help meeee." Then she seemed to melt away and disappear.

The preacher was so overcome with what he had just seen and heard that he collapsed and fell in a faint on the floor. He woke up at sunrise, and everything seemed to be in order. After reading his bible and praying, the preacher decided he must have had a bad dream. For now, he needed to repay the family who had given him shelter.

The girl and her grandparents were having breakfast when they heard the chopping. They went outside to find the preacher swinging a heavy ax next to a big, fresh stack of firewood.

"Perhaps I could persuade you to stay one more night," the grandfather said to the preacher. "This evening, all twelve neighbors in the countryside gather here for a fine feast. You would be most welcome."

When the grandfather had told him twelve neighbors were coming to dinner, the preacher felt a cold chill. He returned to the hearth where he'd seen the woman. He set about removing the stones and then dug down a few inches with his pocketknife.

After a few minutes of digging, the delicate skeleton of a young woman was fully exposed. The preacher carefully broke off the little finger on the left hand and put it in his coat pocket. Later, he walked back across the field to dinner. He placed the finger, unnoticed, on one of the platters of food.

The platter was passed from person to person. Nothing at all happened until it reached the eleventh diner, an average looking fellow who wore glasses. Suddenly, the little finger bone jumped from the plate and wrapped itself around the man's thumb!

Everyone gasped, and some let out screams, as the man shook and shook his thumb, but the bony little finger would not let go! He tried to pull it off, but the bones gripped his thumb like a vise! "Get it off! Get it off!" the man screamed.

"Tell what you did!" the preacher bellowed. "Tell what you did!"

The little finger tightened even more and blood began to run from the man's thumb!

"I killed her!" the man in glasses shouted. "She spurned me, and I murdered her!"

Instantly, the little finger relaxed its grip on the man's thumb. The bony digit fell to the table and went still.

The man in glasses began to sob, "I murdered her and buried her beneath the hearth." More sobs. "I am a murderer." He would later be found guilty of murder and hanged.

The preacher and the grandfather dug a deep grave for the young woman. The preacher put her left little finger back in place before she was placed in a nice coffin made by the grandfather. The next morning, the preacher conducted a service, and the girl and the grandmother placed a cross and flowers on the grave.

The preacher went back to the abandoned house to pick up his few possessions before moving on. As he was leaving, he felt a warm breeze and turned. The young woman floated in front of him. Her eyes were bright and her face was peaceful. She placed her hands on the lapels of the preacher's coat and said softly, "Thank you." Then, smiling, she drifted away and disappeared. The preacher looked down and saw two perfect, snow-white handprints on his lapels.

The preacher traveled the Virginia roads for forty more years preaching his faith. In those four decades, many hundreds of people saw that his coat never frayed, tore, wore out, or even got dirty, no matter how dusty the trail, and that the handprints on his lapel remained blindingly white and perfectly clear.

BLACK INK

JOHN P. HUNTER

I HAVE TRAVELED THE WORLD with my master, and I have learned that life in Paris is in many ways very different from life in London or in Virginia. Yet the lives of servants—and I have been in the service of others for twenty of my thirty years—have much in common. So some here may recognize my tale, though it took place in Paris, as not so foreign to their own experiences.

One thing that all of my station know is that masters will sometimes rant. There is no one thing that sets them off. It could be something as small as an improperly set table or, more seriously, an iron burn on an expensive tablecloth. Occasionally, the master will just be in a foul mood. All of this is part of my daily life and I turn a deaf ear to most of it. Blasphemy, however, I cannot abide, and when it spreads throughout the house in a loud and unrelenting way, I become very uncomfortable. I am presently trying to devise a way to leave, perhaps even to stay here in Virginia. Allow me to tell how this untenable situation came about.

It all began on the evening of a great storm. None of us had ever heard such thunder or seen such lightning. The servant quarters are in the basement so we had thick walls to muffle the sounds. We could only imagine how loud the thunder and bright the lightning flashes must have been upstairs in the master's chamber.

"His new bride must be shaking in her bedclothes," the cook said.

You see, the master had only recently married. His bride is a pleasant woman, but, to be honest, the glow of the wedding is still on her cheeks and who knows what she will be like after a while. At any rate, the master was clearly stricken with his fresh-faced wife and surprised her with new furniture for the house. Their chamber, in particular, was well appointed with a brand new bed, dressing table, desk, and two side chairs that were covered in expensive fabric. All of it sat on a fancy floor covering that coachman said came from the orient.

The newlyweds had gone to sleep before the storm began, but, at the first clap of thunder, the master's eyes flew open. Two more big *booms* and his wife jumped up in bed and let out a frightened cry. Lightning crackled so close to the windows that it filled the room with flashes of light. The thunderclaps came one after another like cannons at a siege.

We could hear the cries of the bride, and they—or his own terror—must have shamed the master to act. As protection, he grabbed a bottle of holy water from the closet, stumbled through the dark, and sprinkled it on his wife, himself, and all over the new bed, furnishings, and carpet. In only a short time, the storm subsided, and all was quiet. The master must have been quite pleased with himself.

At daylight, alas, he turned to look on the lovely face of

his bride and reeled back in shock. Her skin was as black as coal. His own hands and arms were black as was all of the furniture. Even the floor was streaked with wide bands of black!

His wife woke up, took one look at her black skin, her husband, and the room and screeched, "What evil has marred us so?!"

That was the question. Master surmised that somehow the lightning must have scorched them both as well as the furniture.

"But what of the holy water?" his distraught wife wailed. "You said we were safe!"

Before master could reply, I entered the room with their breakfasts. Upon seeing them and the state of the room, I very nearly dropped the entire tray.

Then I noticed an empty bottle by the side of the bed. I picked it up and saw that it was master's ink bottle. The bottle of holy water sat untouched and full on the closet shelf.

When the master realized he had caused the destruction himself by sprinkling man, wife, and furniture with ink, he became enraged. "I am through with the church and all of its practices," he railed.

The man went on and on and continues to do so, even an ocean's voyage later. He has forbidden any talk of religion by his wife or the servants and, worse, rants about the church in a most profane way. The situation has become intolerable for me. Finding a new position will be difficult.

And yet, I would not for a month's wages trade away my memory of that day.

GENTLEMAN ROBBER

JOHN P. HUNTER

I UNDERSTAND A CERTAIN AMOUNT of caution. I, myself, would not try to ford a strange stream without testing its depth, nor would I leave my house filled with burning candles. No, taking precautions is prudent, but, like anything else, it can be taken too far. My former neighbor, Thomas Bainwright, is a case in point.

Thomas was pleasant enough and well-to-do, with several houses around town that he rented or leased to great advantage. He was a good neighbor and, from what I observed, a thoughtful husband and father. He did, however, worry about the safety of his money. This worrying became, I must say, obsessive. "The riffraff," he fumed, "are everywhere. Oh, what a fine world it would be if it were inhabited by gentlemen only."

His wife and my own were good friends, and Mrs. Bainwright once confided to my wife that her husband moved his cash and tobacco notes almost daily. One day it might be hidden under the floorboards. The next day he might lower it down his well in a canvas pouch. Later in the week the money could be behind a brick in the chimney or under hay in the stable. Thomas would rush home several times a day to make sure his gold, silver, and notes were safe. This began to wear on Mrs. Bainwright, and she asked her husband who was it exactly that he feared would steal his money. Well, Mr. Bainwright offered up a list of potential thieves that included pirates, drunkards, desperate orphans, shady gamblers, vagabonds, stray dogs, squirrels, and crows, just to name a few.

No matter what hiding place he thought of, he conjured up a host of reasons why it would not be safe from the lower sort. At last, he decided that the only solution was to keep the money on his person at all times. At least he could then pat it, count it, look at it to make sure it was all intact.

Mrs. Bainwright made her husband a belt with a pouch secured by sturdy buttons on either side and placed half the coins and notes in each one. With the weight evenly distributed and the belt and pouches hidden under his long coat, Mr. Bainwright felt better about his money. He did, however, have to adjust his walk to compensate for the weight.

A month or so later, Mr. Bainwright was riding his horse along a country road after having inspected some land for sale in the area. A well-dressed gentleman on a good horse rode up from behind. The arrival caused Thomas no concern as the man was obviously from refined stock. "And a fine afternoon to you, sir," Mr. Bainwright said.

"And to you, sir," the gentleman replied, "although I fear I have troubling news."

"Pray tell," Bainwright said, concerned.

"Do not be obvious about it, but I ask that you glance over your shoulder and see if a tall man on a black horse is behind us."

Mr. Bainwright was confused but did as the gentleman asked. Sure enough, there was a tall man riding a black horse some distance behind them. "Yes, he is back at the curve in the road near a stand of trees."

"Oh, my," the gentleman said in a distressed voice. "He just robbed me and will no doubt soon ride up and inflict the same mischief on you. His horse is quite fast, and there is no chance of outrunning him."

Mr. Bainwright's fears and insecurities came flooding back. Oh, why, he thought, didn't I leave my money buried, or behind the fireplace, or in the well?

The gentleman could see the distress on Thomas's face and said, "Perhaps there is a solution. Give me your money and I will ride on ahead. Since he has already robbed me, he will let me go. When the robber stops you, there will be nothing for you to give him. We shall then meet at the road house a mile hence, and I will return your money."

"I am greatly in your debt," Bainwright said with relief.

"Not at all," the regal man said. "What are gentlemen for if not to help each other?"

Mr. Bainwright removed his belt and pouches and slipped them over to the gentleman. He, in turn, laid the belt and pouches across the front of his saddle. "The tavern in but a few minutes," he smiled. "There the two of us shall toast this little adventure." With that, the gentleman spurred his horse and soon disappeared around a bend in the road.

Within a minute, the tall man galloped up to Mr. Bainwright and slid his big black horse to a stop.

"There is no reason to cause me harm, "a confident Mr. Bainwright said, "I have no money or valuables."

"Did you talk to the man who rode before me?" the tall man asked.

"Yes, sir," Bainwright responded haughtily. "A gentleman of the highest order."

"Oh, then," the highwayman said. "You are very safe. I give you my word none of my friends will meddle with you now as the gentleman is one of us."

SELLING TEETH

JOHN P. HUNTER

ALTHOUGH REARED IN THE LOCAL parish church, I am not a particularly religious man. My lifelong friend, Isaac, is a fervent believer. Our differences in this area have led to some lively debates over the years. One of my arguments has been that if the Savior is so compassionate, why do so many people live in such misery? The sick, the poor, the deformed . . . to what did he attribute their sorry station? Invariably, Isaac would quote some relevant piece of scripture, adding that "the Lord works in mysterious ways."

A clerk by trade, I simply cannot accept something just because someone says it is true. No, my mind is accustomed to numbers, receipts, and ledger entries that are indisputable. Isaac, on the other hand, is most comfortable with ritualistic ceremony and blind faith.

One afternoon, we were having a particularly heated exchange, and I told Isaac a tale I had heard that very morning. This was the sad story of an orphaned boy named Thomas in bound service to a cruel master. The lad arrived at the house of a Mistress Harris with his master, a monster that treated his charges worse than dogs. The boy took the abuse, as his father was dead, his mother nearly so, and his brothers starving. After the parish found him a place in his master's home, he was one less mouth to feed.

While the master smoked a pipe and hurled insults and threats at Thomas, the boy did all of the work. After some time, Mistress Harris returned from shopping and inspected the work. The chimney practically sparkled and, of course, the master took full credit while berating the boy for his lazy ways. Mistress Harris nodded in sympathy. She had experienced servant problems of her own.

Then she noticed something interesting about Thomas. Against all odds, the young man had a set of straight white teeth. A surgeon in town had experienced some recent success implanting teeth from one person into another, and Mistress Harris's husband was in desperate need of some new ones. "Young man," she asked Thomas, "would you be interested in selling some of your teeth?"

The master jumped right in., "Of course! He would be most happy to accommodate your needs! He was just telling me how he had teeth to spare!"

"So we can arrange a transaction?" Madam Harris asked.

"The boy is slow, so I will handle the business in his interest," the master said. He surveyed the fine house, her clothes, and jewelry, and settled on a figure he supposed she could afford.

"This lad is like a son to me," the master said, "and I would like him to seize an opportunity when it presents itself. After much consideration, I believe the following proposition to be fair . . . for the sum of three guineas, you may choose the two teeth you most admire."

After only a minute of haggling, Mistress Harris agreed. She sent a servant to fetch a tooth drawer, who returned with the instrument. Shaking with fear, Thomas opened his mouth wide. Mistress Harris inspected his teeth as if she were looking at apples in the market.

"That one and that one," she said indicating two particularly white and robust teeth.

Without a moment's hesitation, the tooth drawer clamped down on one of the teeth and out it came. Thomas yelped with pain and then again. The second tooth was pulled.

As Thomas moaned and tried to wipe away the blood with his sleeve, his master accepted the three guineas from the lady and put them into his own pocket. As the woman excitedly inspected the new teeth for her husband, the master bade his customer a gracious farewell and grabbed Thomas's arm. They took their leave.

They stopped at a shop and the master, with great flourish, bought Thomas a pair of cheap silver buckles for his battered shoes. The ornaments cost less than a tenth of a guinea.

At this point in my telling of the story, Isaac blurted out, "Why, that is horrible! Selling his teeth! The Lord will punish that man for taking such advantage of the boy."

"I doubt that," I responded. "You see, evil runs roughshod over the helpless, and religion helps them not at all."

There was only one way to resolve this dispute. Off we went in search of the master chimney sweep. It did not take us long as the tavern keepers knew him well. They directed us to his squalid hovel.

There we found a thin woman sitting outside with a faraway look in her eye. We inquired about the man and she said in a detached way, "He is my husband. Not three hours ago, he came home with his pockets full of money. Over two guineas he had. He changed his clothes and went out to buy a gallon of beer."

"You see!" I said to Isaac. "The man is out celebrating!"

"Not quite," the thin woman said with a slight smile. "When he got the change from the guinea, one of the coins was bent. He put that in his mouth while he counted the others. Somehow, the bent coin got lodged in his throat and he has been suffocating ever since. The doctor says he will surely die."

Isaac simply nodded.

THE LITTLE SHEPHERD

JOHN P. HUNTER

BEHIND CLOSED DOORS, MRS. GOLDING was a most unpleasant woman. Out and about, she was as sweet as pie. Shopkeepers knew they would be entertained by her wit and graciousness. Her friends often felt shamed by the self-less way in which Mrs. Golding helped the unfortunate. To a one, members of her parish church thought there could not be a more openhearted, kind, and gentle woman on earth. No one could have suspected her secret . . . Mrs. Golding had a horrific, terrifying temper.

Unfortunately for Mr. Golding, all of his wife's rage was directed at him. By the time Mrs. Golding returned home after a full day of smiling at orphans, she was ready to explode. Mr. Golding would rush home from his job as a clerk in the courts, hoping to arrive before his wife. That gave him a few minutes to try and make sure everything was in its place. A candleholder out of place, a curtain slightly askew, a speck of dust on a table, or even a dead petunia in the garden was enough to set her off. When Mr. Golding heard the door open, his stomach tightened into knots and ands began to shake, with good reason.

The epithets spewed forth. Years before, Mr. Golding had given up trying to defend himself. His wife's eyes would be so full of crazed anger that, like some animals, Mr. Golding chose to play dead. Mr. Golding was a physically frail man and really would have stood no chance against his robust wife.

Eventually, Mrs. Golding would begin to wind down. She would straighten her clothes, take a small glass of wine, and begin admiring her prized collection of china, pewter, brass, and earthenware. Mr. Golding would go to the small cellar and work on his miniature ships by candlelight. The vessels were only a foot or so long, but the craftsmanship and detail were extraordinary. It was as if a selection of naval and merchant ships had been lifted from the Yorktown port, shrunk down, and placed on Mr. Golding's workbench. He worked late into the night cutting and shaving each tiny timber just so, stringing rigging at precise angles and sewing tiny sails.

One afternoon, the courts were adjourned early and unexpectedly. Ah, Mr. Golding thought, extra time to get the house in order. He hurried home and meticulously cleaned and straightened everything. He was sure the house had never looked better and could not see anything that would trigger her ire. As he turned to admire his work, the tail of his coat knocked a small earthenware shepherd, one of his wife's prized Staffordshire figures, from a shelf, and the staff broke on the floor. Panicked, Mr. Golding used some of the glue for his models and reattached the staff. It was a perfect job. He placed it in its exact spot on the shelf just as his wife turned the doorknob.

Mrs. Golding made a turn of the house. She stopped at the Staffordshire figures, but, thankfully, did not notice anything untoward with the little shepherd. Reentering the main room, she said to her husband, "Go play with your little ships. I am exhausted and certainly have no need of your company." Compared to what she said most nights, that was a love poem.

An hour later, Mr. Golding was so focused on carving a small mast that he did not hear his wife's footsteps coming down the cellar steps. The door flew open, and Mrs. Golding stood glaring with rage. As a boy, Mr. Golding had seen a rabid dog in the woods and, to him, his wife looked every bit as deranged. Her eyes were wide and brimmed with bright red, and spittle spewed from her snarling mouth and gathered as foam at the corners. Her entire body was shaking with fury.

"You sniveling worm!" the big woman rasped. "You will pay for breaking my shepherd!"

With that, Mrs. Golding lurched at her husband and grabbed the small man by the neck, lifted him off the ground, and then flung him against the workbench. Mr. Golding pleaded, "It was an accident! Just an accident!"

Oblivious to his cries, the crazed woman smashed to smithereens every one of his ships. "No!" Mr. Golding yelled. "Not my ships!" It was too much for the man and he charged his wife, grabbing her by the neck.

Instead of slowing her down, the attack fueled her wrath. Mrs. Golding ripped her husband's small hands from her throat, picked him up over her head, and slammed him to the floor. Then she stared down at her dead husband.

At the funeral service, Mrs. Golding was the picture of wifely grief. Her friends commented on how bravely she was handling the tragedy of her dear husband's fall down the cellar steps. There was a constant stream of sympathizers at the Golding home after the funeral. Throughout it all, the widow exuded just the right amount of sadness, sense of loss, and resolve to somehow carry on. Late in the evening, the last mourner finally left, and Mrs. Golding was free to admire her earthenware, china, brass, and pewter piece by piece.

Suddenly, a fine china plate flew off the shelf, sailed across the room, and crashed into the fireplace. Then another.

"Stop this! Stop this!" Mrs. Golding screamed as several earthenware figures rose from the table and then smashed into the floor.

The brass pieces soared across the room and embedded themselves into the wall. The pewter plates and tea service hurled themselves into the flames in the fireplace.

Mrs. Golding was furious and screeched, "Show yourself! Show yourself! I will beat you like a mongrel dog!"

At that moment, a particularly delicate and almost paper-thin china bread plate left the shelf and whipped across the room at such velocity that it severed Mrs. Golding's head as cleanly as a surgeon's scalpel.

The next morning, Mrs. Golding's neighbor, Mr. Gresham, dropped by to check on the grieving widow. Receiving no answer to his knock, and concerned, Mr. Gresham entered the house and cautiously made his way into the main parlor. The scene that greeted him very nearly made Mr. Gresham lose his senses. Separated from her body, Mrs. Golding's head lay against the wall. Every single one of her treasures was either smashed, broken, burned, or hopelessly bent.

Except for a little earthenware shepherd that sat serenely on the mantle.

THE GHOSTLY DRUMMER BOY

RUTH TSCHAN

ONE OF MY FAVORITES STORIES my papa used to tell was about a ghostly drummer boy. Seems this ghostie boy first made his presence known to Sir John Maupassant at his country place of Tedworth over there nigh unto Londontown.

Well, Sir John got wind of the fact that a drummer boy was drumming on the street corner in a nearby village and folks was coming by and dropping coins into his hat. There ain't nothing wrong with that, you understand—except the boy was working with a forged permit. Now we all know a forged permit ain't no more good than the scrap of paper it be writ upon. Why the lad would ever have done such a thing I can't rightly tell you, but so it were.

Well, Sir John weren't going to have that, no siree! So he got on his horse and got the constable and off they rode to the village to see for themselves what was going on over there.

Sure enough there was the boy drumming away, and folks was enchanted. They say he were such a comely lad, blond curly hair to his shoulders, bright blue eyes, and such a smile you never want to see! And that drum! It were the prettiest drum you ever did see. It were pale, shiny, ash wood, trimmed in scarlet paint with little gold tassels on the sides. There he was drumming away and those little gold tassels just a-bobbin'. He was holding them folks in the palm of his hand.

Well, Sir John had the lad arrested and hauled off to the magistrate, and before you know it, he had been condemned to hard labor in the islands. Now, we all know just about how long a man lasts when he's been condemned to the islands, what with the bugs and the heat and the hard labor. Well, it pains me greatly to tell you this, but the comely lad very soon gave up the ghost—he died.

There sat the constable back in Londontown with the beautiful drum, with the scarlet trim and the little gold tassels. He didn't quite know what to do with it, so he decided to bundle it up and send it over to Sir John at Tedworth.

Well, let me tell you! Sir John had no more than got that drum in the house when his troubles began. In the dead of the night it would start, deep in the bowels of Tedworth, a rumbling and a drummin'—up it would come through the house, up the staircase, getting louder and louder as it come. Drummin' and drummin' and drummin'. You never knew whose room it would end up in. Ended up in the children's room one night. Well, Sir John's serving man heard all the commotion and he decided he had better go see what was going on. So he crept up the stairs and opened the door to the children's room just enough to peek in.

What he saw was an astonishment! Well, I should say it was what he *didn't* see that was the astonishment. There were the children marching round and round the room and the drum just a drummin'—those little gold tassels a-bobbin'.

But—there weren't no head, and there weren't no feet, and, sure enough, there weren't no hands. And one of the drumsticks was a piece of kindling wood off the hearthside.

Well, the serving man plucked up his courage and threw open the door and said, "You, there! Stop that infernal racket! You're scaring these children to death."

Let me tell you! In that boy's lifetime he had had a *good* mama. She had brung him up right. When he was told to stop, he stopped! The children ran on off down the passage in search of Nanny, as they were in need of a little comforting. And the serving man said, "Hand me that piece of kindling wood!" Very polite little ghostie boy he was, he handed over the kindling wood. Well, there stood the serving man holding the piece of kindling wood. He didn't quite know what he should do with it—didn't have sense enough to put it back on the hearthside, you understand. So he handed it back to the ghostie boy. The ghostie boy thought, well, this is a good game to play. So he handed it back to the serving man. Back and forth and back and forth it went. They might have been playing this silly game to this very night if Sir John hadn't walked in.

Sir John took one look and said, "Ho, there! Stop that ungodly game and you, there, go on about your business." Well, the serving man hurried on off, and the ghostie boy just faded back into the shadows. BUT—not before leaving behind one last parting insult! Peeuh! Such a stink! You wouldn't believe the stink some ghosties give off. Well, Sir John ripped out his lace handkerchief from his sleeve, threw it over his nose, backed out of that room, and slammed the door behind him. You know, they say he never would go in that wing of Tedworth again!

And do you think that were the end of that ghostie boy? No indeed! It weren't a fortnight 'til he were back again. Every night, all night long, drummin' and drummin'. The family weren't getting a wink of sleep, they were out of their minds! Finally, one night, Sir John got up and said, "Come on, Lady Maupassant, gather up the children, we're leaving here." They had fourteen children, you understand. Well, she gathers them all up, the least one out of his cradle, and off they go to a neighbor's house. The neighbor very kindly took them in, gave the children some hot chocolate—everybody didn't have chocolate, you understand, it were very rare and very dear, so that were a fine thing to do for those frightened children—and gave Sir John and Lady Maupassant a glass of wine. Sir John was walking up and down, up and down, with his glass of wine, and finally he set it down and he said, "Come on, Lady Maupassant, get the children together, we're going home—I'm not going to let some ghostie boy drive me out of house and home!" Well, I ask you—what do you think she said to that? Uh, huh! "Not this night we're not," she said. So he said, "All right I'll go by myself." Off he went, up the stairs, tucked himself in and pulled up the covers. He was going to have a good night's sleep.

Oh, no! There it was—right at the foot of Sir John's bed! Drummin' and drummin', and those little gold tassels just a-bobbin'. Well, Sir John sat up and said, "You, there! If you be of the Devil you pound three times!" Three times he pounded on the boot of the bed! Well, let me tell you! Sir John was out of that bed, into his pants, grabbed his coat and was out of there before you could say "scat"—he were so afrightened! He went down into town in search of Reverend Adair to have the reverend come and bless the place, get rid of that ghostie boy once and for all.

Any of you ever had the Reverend Adair come to your house to get rid of any unwanted spirits? Well, I'm so glad you never needed him, but if ever you should, he's a good man. Well, he come. And he went on up to the children's room, hid himself in the shadows of the bed furniture—all still and quiet—to wait. Didn't have long to wait—pretty soon there it were—a-drummin' and a-drummin'—getting louder and louder and coming closer and closer. And there it were right in the room with him. And there were a scratching and a scratching at the window light and it were as though some great beastie had got in and flung itself upon the children's bed—and there were that stink again, such a smell! The Reverend Adair is not readily affrighted, but all that worthy gentleman wanted was to get out of there—not without blessing the children's room first, of course!

Out he went and down into the town, and he spread the word—there is surely a ghost at Tedworth, and I know not what to do about it.

But the strangest part of this tale is this—you know about the good Dr. Benjamin Franklin up there in Philadelphia? Well, he has the newspaper, the *Pennsylvania Gazette*. Not a fortnight ago he had an article in the *Gazette* that said that self-same ghostie lad had found his way across the great water and was to this very day walking the length and breadth of these colonies. Me thinks a word to the wise would not be amiss here. You going to be out and about this eventide—it's dark in them streets now—you just look sharp in the bushes and keep your ears peeled—you just might hear that drummer boy a-drummin' or catch sight of that beautiful little drum with the scarlet trim and the little gold tassels.

But you ain't going to see no head, and you ain't going to see no feet, and you sure enough ain't going to see no hands.

DEAD MAN'S GRIP

GAYNELLE McNICHOLS

DOWN IN YORKTOWN, YEARS AGO, just as today, the men liked to spend their evenings in the taverns. They favored an establishment under the hill on the waterfront. They'd gather there of an evening and drink a pint or two and then talk of all that was happening around the town. Now, at this particular time, all the talk was of something that had happened a few weeks before over in Williamsburg. There'd been a hanging of a man from Yorktown for the terrible crime of murder. They brought his body back to Yorktown and buried him in the cemetery on the hill above the town. Of course, with him being a murderer and all, they buried him in a far corner of the cemetery away from good Christian folks.

That night in the tavern, the men spoke of strange things that had been happening in that cemetery—strange lights hovering over the murderer's grave, strange sounds coming from the far corner of the cemetery at the stroke of midnight. One of the men said, "I believe that Satan inhabits that grave where the murderer lies."

As they talked on, one of the men, a gambling man, spoke up and said, "I'll wager a pretty penny, a purse of silver, if any of you will go to the murderer's grave after the stroke of midnight." Things grew quiet, and not a man in the tavern took him up on his wager. Then, from over in the corner near the fireplace, a voice spoke up.

"I'll take you up on your wager. I fear nothing in that cemetery. I fear neither God nor the Devil." 'Twas the voice of Samuel Cobb, a young ne'er-do-well.

Money was tossed on the tables and the bets were made. A plan was contrived. At the stroke of midnight, Samuel would go up the hill to the cemetery alone and approach the murderer's grave. He would take with him a hammer and a wooden stake. He was to drive that stake into the grave. On the morrow, his friends would see the stake as proof Samuel had been there, and he'd win the purse of silver.

Once the clock stuck midnight, up the hill Samuel went. His friends walked with him as far as the churchyard gate. As Samuel bade them a good evening, he laughed, "You fools, you great fools! You might as well have tossed all your money in the York River. Tomorrow evening, I shall be spending that money in the Bunch of Grapes tavern, toasting you for the fools that you are."

With that, Samuel turned his back on them and walked down the churchyard path. 'Twas a cold, dark night with the wind whistling through the trees high on that hill above Yorktown. Samuel pulled his great coat close about him. He walked and walked until he found the murderer's burial place. Samuel strode boldly over to the mound of dirt and drove the stake into the murderer's grave.

"What fools those fellows are," he said out loud. "Don't they know I fear nothing? I've made quick work of this and shall soon be home, warm and snug in my bed."

With that, Samuel attempted to rise from atop the grave, but *he could not move!* He felt the cold, clammy hands of the dead man holding him fast, pulling him down! "Oh, Lord!" he screamed. "The murderer's got me! He's going to pull me into the grave and on down into Hell itself! Help me, oh, help me," he cried as his voice faded. Then there was silence. And there was silence all the rest of the night but for the wind whistling through the trees high on that hill above Yorktown.

Early the next morning, Samuel's friends went to his home. His mother opened the door to their knock. "I've not seen him," she said. "And I fear some harm has come to my son."

Samuel's friends quickly ran to the cemetery. One of them ran ahead. Soon they heard him cry out, "Here he is! I've found him! Here he lies!"

The others rushed toward their friend's voice and saw Samuel lying cold and dead atop the murderer's grave. His face was frozen in sheer, paralyzed horror! As they prepared to remove Samuel's body and take it back to his mother, they discovered what had frightened him to death. It wasn't the cold, clammy hands of a dead man but Samuel's pride that had killed him. In his haste to get home and prove his friends wrong, he had paid no attention to what he was doing. Samuel had taken the stake and driven it through the tail of his great coat and that is what held him fast!

BLACKBEARD'S COURTSHIP

JASON WHITEHEAD

THERE WAS IN NORTH CAROLINA a young lady named Miss Eden. She was so beautiful that she caught the eye of a particular suitor who, one day, showed up at her doorstep offering a bag of silver coins. He asked for nothing in return for those coins except her hand in marriage. She refused. The next week, he came back again with the silver coins and a bag of gold coins as well. Again, he asked for nothing in return except her hand in marriage, and again she refused. The third week, he came back offering the silver coins, the gold coins, and a small box filled with diamonds and rubies. Miss Eden said she had no intention of marrying any man she did not love. What she did not say was that she was already in love with someone else, a man named Phillip.

Phillip was rather young in life and could not offer Miss Eden such gifts. In fact, he couldn't provide her with much of a life at all, but they were in love and that was all that mattered to Miss Eden. That is, aside from the obvious. For, do not all women who intend to spend the rest of their lives with but one man also prefer him to be pleasing to their eyes?

Of course, and no one would have found that first man pleasing to anything. They say he stood near on seven foot tall, weighing nearly four hundred pounds. A huge, barrel-shaped man who smelled of something that had died three weeks ago. And if that weren't bad enough, this man also went about the city unshaven. The man, in fact, wore a beard that started right below his eyes and then tangled and gnarled its nasty way well past his waist. So famous, in fact, were the black whiskers upon his face that, if you saw this man on the streets, you did not say, "Oh, good day, Mr. Teach." No, if you called him anything, it was more likely his more common name . . . Blackbeard.

Now, all have heard of Blackbeard, so how do you suppose he was getting all of the wonderful things he was offering Miss Eden? By pirating, pillaging, robbing, stealing, killing men, and sinking ships. Do you suppose, however, he was going through all of that trouble to give her those things because he was in love with Miss Eden? Not Blackbeard. For as beautiful as she was, he had his eyes on a prize of a different sort. Miss Eden was the daughter of the most powerful, wealthiest, most influential man in all of North Carolina. This was Governor Eden, the governor of the colony of North Carolina.

With the governor as his father-in-law, Blackbeard could expect every port, town, and acre of land within those borders to be safe for him and his crew. That is what he desired and that is what Miss Eden denied him, time after time. In fact, she grew so frustrated with the advances upon her that one day she decided she had had enough. She called in her servants to pack up all of her belongings. She had those belongings loaded upon a wagon, and she had them and herself carried off to the west to be hidden away from this pirate.

Blackbeard was the kind of fellow used to having his way. He paced back and forth upon the deck of his ship, trying to figure out where she had gone and how to bring her back. He decided to send some of his men ashore to find out what they could by whatever means.

When those men returned a while later, they brought with them some useful information. You see, they had found out about Phillip. They told Blackbeard where the man lived. Blackbeard went up to Phillip's door and knocked. When the young man answered, he was frightened. He knew who stood before him. Who wouldn't recognize that beast of a man with the mass of hair upon his face? Yet, the pirate proved himself a gentleman. "You have no need for fear this day for I have not come to harm you. In truth, I have come to right a harm I have already committed. You see, I have found out that you and I both love the same lady, yet she has chosen your heart over mine. As a way of removing myself from this competition, I invite you, sir, to dine with me this evening on board my ship."

Phillip was no fool. He knew what would happen to him when he stepped on board the *Queen Anne's Revenge*. Yet who wouldn't have the slightest bit of curiosity to see what treasure lay on board the pirate ship? The curiosity was so strong in Phillip that it caused him to say yes.

But again, Phillip was no fool. He put a small pistol, well loaded and placed at the half cock, within his waistcoat pocket. When he arrived on board, he found this precaution to be unnecessary for the pirate still proved himself a gentleman. Blackbeard invited Phillip onto the deck of his ship, even invited Phillip into his cabin. When Phillip walked into Blackbeard's cabin, he saw before his eyes treasures that he could only have imagined. There was gold and silver trim around the walls. Beautiful furniture was set all about the room. In the center, a large dining table was laid out with every means of beast and fish and fruit and fowl, and of course, rum. For what is a proper meal without a proper toast, "To her Majesty, Queen Anne"? A toast that was washed down with more toasts, to her majesty's children . . . one by one. All thirteen.

It was not long before Phillip found himself well within his cups, a state he was quite unfamiliar with. His chair became a device that would merely keep him from tumbling to the floor. The pirate, seeing his opportunity, arose from his chair, walked all the way around the table, never taking his eyes off of Phillip. He walked up to Phillip and looked him from head to toe and demanded, "Sir, you will this evening tell me who your tailor is!"

Blackbeard reached an arm out to Phillip's shoulder. "Most impressive is your sleeve, which begins innocently enough here at the shoulder but ends down at the cuff with stitching so small you can barely see it with the unassisted eye."

Then, while holding Phillip's wrist with one hand, the pirate reached behind his back, withdrew an awful knife and, in one quick turn, took Phillip's hand from his arm. Phillip began to grab for that pistol in his pocket. It fell harmlessly upon the floor. The pirate called for his men to take Phillip outside, cut him into little pieces, and throw him over as food for the fish.

There sat Miss Eden, waiting week after week for any news from her beloved Phillip. One particular Tuesday, she noticed a rider approaching from the east. He was wearing the livery of her father's house and he was bringing with him a package. The package was delivered, brought up to her room, and set on the table beside her. Miss Eden wondered what was inside. It had to be a gift, a token of Phillip's love, but what could it be? Perhaps a new pin for her hat, she thought. Or maybe a brooch for her gown. Or possibly, she hoped, a ring for her finger. She removed the paper wrapping, opened the wooden lid, and found inside nothing except for Phillip's dead, severed hand upon a red silk pillow. Though that is not entirely true, for there was one more thing, a small note clutched betwixt those lifeless fingers that, when removed, simply revealed the words "You wished for his hand . . . and now you have it."

WHERE THE GHOST DOG RAN

RUTH TSCHAN

MANY, MANY YEARS AGO, there were Indians here-abouts. There was one old Indian chief, Chief Running Deer, who was getting on in years, but he still loved nothing better than to walk the length and breadth of this beautiful colony. He would come by our place—he knew he was always welcome—and sit under the old Sycamore tree in the front yard. My papa would come out and share a pipe of tobacco with him, and all of us children would sit about as close to the old man as we could get because he always had a good tale to tell. My favorite was about the great ghost dog in a Cherokee village.

In the village lived an old man with long, flowing white hair and his little wife who was as old—she looked like a shriveled up apple. They made their living grinding corn into cornmeal to make cornmeal mush and cornbread and such. He would take the cornmeal around the village and trade it with his friends and relatives for whatever they needed—maybe a nice piece of deerskin to make a jacket or a haunch of a bear to put in the stewpot of an evening.

The cornmeal was kept in big stone jars to protect it.

One morning, the old man went out to get his meal, and something or somebody had dumped over one of those big jars. There was cornmeal all over the place. Most of it was gone. The old man was perplexed. He couldn't understand who would come in the night and take all his meal. It couldn't have been anyone from the village. You don't go around stealing from your friends and relatives. You don't go around stealing from anybody, now do you?

The old man cast about to see if he could discover what had gone on in the night. Maybe there was a scratch in the sand or a broken branch on a bush. He found something all right—he found a pawprint. That pawprint was so big—it was as big as your mama's tea table! No human dog ever made a paw print that big. It had to have been a ghost.

The old man decided to go down into the village and gather all the elders, the wise men of the tribe, to see what could be done about this. One by one, the elders stood up and offered their suggestions. One by one, the old man just shook his head and said, "No, son. Sit down. We can't do that."

You see, the Cherokees have a deep reverence for anything in the Great Circle of Life put in place by the Great Spirit. In that Circle of Life, there are the folks and the critters and the ghostly beasties. Now the old man didn't want the ghostly beasty hurt and, I would hasten to assure you, he didn't want it upset. You haven't had trouble on your hands 'til you've had an upset ghost! So, what was there to do?

Then the old man stood up and a hush fell over the whole tribe. They respected the old man for his white hair but also for his wisdom. "This," he said, "is what we should do. Twilight time, when the shadows has fell, all of you come to the lodge. Bring all your noise makers—drums, strings of seashells you can shake and rattle, big old gourds with the dried seeds you can shake and rattle. We'll all hide quietly in the bushes until the great beast appears. Then we'll jump out, make a great racket, and scare him away. He'll never trouble the Cherokees again."

That sounded like a good idea. So, come twilight time, they all gathered quietly in the bushes around the lodge. They didn't have to wait long. Pretty soon, one of the little Indian boys said, "There it comes!"

This great ghostly thing was coming across the fields and through the woods. It was the most fearsome apparition you'd ever want to clap your eyes upon. That child tucked his head in his mama's lap and held on to her skirts for dear life! The thing just kept coming and coming, right down to where they ground the corn. It sniffed about and loped on over to the big jars and dumped one over with its great paw. He was gobbling up the meal with his great big mouth.

Do you think there was a sound out of any one of those Indian braves? They were petrified, not moving a muscle. Then the old man began to make noise with his drum and his feet and his mouth. Seeing how brave he was, they all joined in and made a great racket—rattling, shaking, shouting, and stomping their feet.

Well, even ghosties can be scared right out of their wits. That poor dog's ears were back against his head, his tail between his legs, and he started running round and round in that circle of Indians. He couldn't find a way to escape.

Finally, he just gathered up all the strength in those great hind legs and made one tremendous leap right over the heads of all those Indians and went racing off across the night sky, corn meal coming out of his mouth all the way. It looked just like one great shining roadway across the night sky all paved with diamonds and sparkling.

One of the little Indian girls looked up, pointed, and said, "Gilli ut sun sta nuni," "where the great ghost dog ran." And that is what you will hear Indian children say to this day, "Gilli ut sun sta nuni," "where the great ghost dog ran." When you go out, look at the night sky, and see that great splash of stars sparkling away up there, you call it something else . . . The Milky Way.

THE HOUSEGUEST

DONNA WOLF

SOME THINK ME MOST ILL MANNERED as I've not the habit of allowing guests in after dark. I like my privacy. 'Tis safer that way, especially for a woman alone. There is more to it, of course. Much more! Otherwise, people would think me only cautious, not daft. Aye, daft they call me! And whisper and point as I walk these streets.

They say now that Mr. Paul is dead, all is well, and there is nothing to fear. But I know the truth. For I saw Mr. Paul with mine own eyes and heard the truth from his very lips.

It all began when I still worked for Mr. Greenhow in his shop. Mr. Paul was the most genteel of men. He had a ready smile and always took the time to pass discourse with me. If truth be told, I found him most pleasing to look upon. Most tall and straight, with even teeth, hair neatly queued. 'Twas his habit to wear a yellow waistcoat that glittered and shined in the sun.

For nigh on three years, Mr. Paul rode in from the County of York every second Thursday of the month. And 'twas April last he first made mention of a traveler who knocked upon his door late one eve asking to be allowed to take his ease for the night. He said this stranger had a most peculiar manner of speaking.

Then came May and I noticed poor Mr. Paul seemed out of sorts. Pale of the face and acted in a distracted manner. When I inquired after his health he said he was merely tired but was altogether well. When I asked him what became of his houseguest, and I found this most odd, he tells me that this man had yet to leave his house. When I asked Mr. Paul why the delay in departure, he got a far-off look in his eyes and did not answer.

June is such a time for people in and out of this city that it wasn't until the month's end that I realized I had not had the pleasure of Mr. Paul's company. And when July's heat had settled over us, again Mr. Paul remained absent. I did not see Mr. Paul again until an unusually cool and rainy day in August. And such a change! I did not recognize him at first glance.

I was returning to Mr. Greenhow's after dinner when I saw a man walking slowly up the street. I had almost dismissed him from my mind when I caught a glimpse of a yellow waistcoat. 'Twas no longer clean and well pressed but dirt-encrusted, and it looked like it had not parted from the body in a many a week.

I called out, "Mr. Paul?" When he turned his face fully to me, it was indeed Mr. Paul, though such a state he was in! His skin was pulled tight over his skull, hair mussed and filled with leaves and twigs as if he had slept in the wood. His eyes were dark and sunk deep in their sockets, and they looked so very empty. But what drew my eyes were his teeth. To this day I pray I was mistaken, but it seemed to me his teeth did not sit properly in his mouth.

I asked him what plagued him so and very quietly he said it was the stranger he took in. He was a vampire! To my shame, I laughed. Mr. Paul grabbed me by both arms and hissed in my face that 'twas no laughing matter! He was most tormented night after night. He looked me square in the eye and said he was damned for all eternity and was on his way to Bruton Parish to find salvation for his soul. That was the last time I ever saw Mr. Paul alive.

When Mr. Paul laid his hand upon the parish door, his skin began to blacken and smoke and sizzle like hot fat upon the griddle! He clutched at his burning skin, clawed at his eyes, and expired there upon the stairs of our church.

'Twas but a month gone by when the stories made their way here. Of how several persons in the County of York swore Mr. Paul stood outside their windows on the darkest of nights begging to be allowed in. Near every morning, some frightened citizen relayed a similar tale. They said the voice outside in the dark was so tortured and tormented that no person of sound mind would have considered granting the man entry.

A committee of learned men, including our own doctor of the town, went to Mr. Paul's grave. To err on the side of caution, they took along a wooden stake and mallet, the only thing said capable of killing a vampire. By the light of the torch, they unearthed his poor remains.

They took up his body, which had been dead and buried for thirty days. It was as if no death or interment had transpired. They found Mr. Paul to be fresh and free of corruption! As they watched, Mr. Paul bled from the eyes, ears, nose, and mouth a most florid blood. His death shroud was all over bloody and his finger and toenails had grown until they looked like beast's claws.

'Twas the good doctor who drove the stake through

the body's heart. It's said what had been Mr. Paul gave a shudder and a most horrid groan. Wasting no time at all, they burnt poor Mr. Paul's body to ashes and placed them back in his grave. The men of the committee wiped the dust from their hands, breathed a sigh of great relief, and said 'twas a task well done!

All is well and there is nothing to fear, they all say. Ha! Then who, pray tell, *taps* and *scratches* upon my window night after night?

THE GAMBLE

JAN COUPERTHWAITE

I AM MRS. EMMALINE POWERS, and I live here in Williamsburg. I have just come in from Richmondtown visiting with my oldest and dearest friend, Catharine Gamble. We have known each other since we were little girls, growing up together in the Shenandoah Valley here in Virginia.

Catharine was always a special girl and is still a special woman to this day. She has the ability to see into the future with her dreams. Now, most folks were plum afraid of her because of her dreams, but I never was. I knew a lot of her dreams didn't come true. I learned this after we acted on a few with terrible results.

I'll never forget the time we were about fourteen tobacco seasons. She came to me and said, "Emmy. I've had a dream. I know where Mrs. Harris has misplaced her pearl ring."

"Mrs. Harris told us if we found her ring we were supposed to give it right back to her," I said.

Catharine looked at me and said, "Oh pooh! You know what they say, 'finders is keepers.' So, are you going to help me get the ring or not?"

According to Catharine's dream, the ring was in a cherry pie made by Mrs. Harris, and we intended to get it. There was a church sociable the very next day, and Mrs. Harris always brought her prize cherry pie. When we got to the sociable, Mrs. Harris's delicious-looking pie was sitting on the table. When nobody was looking, we took that pie and ran out the back of the church and up a hill where nobody could see us.

Our plan was to put the pie back on the table like nothing had happened. I was going to place just my finger on top of the crust and poke a hole down into the filling. I'd worm my finger around, and if I didn't find her ring there, then I'd poke another hole in the crust and keep doing the same thing until I found it. That way, we could get the ring without making a mess.

When I poked my finger in the third time, my hands crashed down through the crust and right into that slimy bloodred filling. Well, I wasn't thinking and jerked out my hands, which sent crust and cherry pie sailing up in the air. Then it came down all over us.

What a mess! Cherry juice was dripping off our caps, lying in our laps, and running down my arms. We were a sight to behold.

We looked at each other and started to laugh. After quite a bit of giggling and carrying on, we began to look all over for Mrs. Harris's ring. Soon, we realized the ring hadn't been in the pie after all, which made us laugh that much harder. After we finally got ourselves under control, I looked down and saw shoes, men's shoes. Then I looked up and up and up. Who should be staring down at us but Reverend Harris? He wasn't smiling. You could say that he had caught us redhanded with his wife's cherry pie.

So, as I said, not all of Catharine's dreams played out exactly as she saw them. I only wish the one I am about to tell you about had not played out at all.

When we were in our later teen years, Catharine's parents moved them out to the western part of Virginia, and we kept in touch with letters. She sent me a letter saying she knew everything about her future husband except his name from a dream. By the time I got her next letter, she not only had met him but was engaged to the man. She said he matched her dream perfectly and his name was Robert Gamble.

We had heard of Robert Gamble in the valley. He was rich and handsome, and he was also a war hero. According to my Momma, however, his flaw was that he gambled. He would bet on just about anything. Catharine's parents didn't seem to mind, so Catharine and Robert were married and started a big family. Through the years, Robert became very wealthy and built Catharine a big mansion right there in Richmondtown. They were so happy.

Then, I got a letter from her asking me to come as soon as I could.

"Emmy," she said after I'd rushed to her side, "I had one of my dreams. It scared me so. I saw Robert happily riding through Richmondtown. Suddenly, his horse reared up, Robert fell out of the saddle, hit his head on a rock, and died right there in the street."

She knew if she was going to save her husband's life, she couldn't let him leave the house. Robert was not the kind of man who put any stock in dreams and such, but she was frantic.

Robert came into the room and said, "Catharine, you look like you've seen a ghost."

"No," she replied, "but I have seen the specter of death,

and it's on you. If you leave this house today, we will never see you alive again."

"Is this one of your dreams?" he asked, and she admitted it was.

Robert said, "I have more faith in my luck than I do in your dreams. I'm even willing to bet you that I'll be back at two of the clock today."

Catharine pleaded with him not to leave the house, but Robert dismissed her concerns and kissed her good-bye. She was standing at that front door as he was leaving and cried, "If you love us, you won't go."

Just before two of the clock, she heard the sound of Robert's horse coming up toward the mansion. Catharine's face lit up. She looked as if a giant weight had lifted off her shoulders.

Then, she heard the creak and the moan of a wagon. She couldn't bear to look out the window, so she told one of her house slaves to do it. He pulled back the blind and looked out.

"Ma'm, it's some men from town and they've got Master Gamble's horse, but he's nowhere in sight," he said.

She rose from her chair and gathered her family around her. They all went out into the garden, and it wasn't long before the wagon came around the side of the mansion. Catharine saw Robert's saddled but riderless horse. She prayed that Robert would be amongst the men, but there was no sign of her husband. As the wagon drew closer, she could see something in the back that sent a chill down her spine. There was a form covered with a blanket and, even from a distance, she could see blood. Tears were streaming down the faces of the men, and she knew something terrible had happened.

The wagon came to a stop. The men jumped out and

ran up to her. They looked with surprise at Catharine and her children who were dressed in black. The men were speechless, but, finally, one gentleman said, "Mrs. Gamble, we don't understand. Who came and told you that Robert was killed today?"

She said, "No one, no one at all. I have dreams that often come true, but Robert never listened to them. I told him of a dream I had last night . . . that if he left the house today, we would never see him alive again. He didn't listen to me then either. He did bet me, though, that he would be back by two of the clock."

Then she took out her watch. It was exactly two of the clock.

"I suppose he won his bet," Catharine said.

I won't speak ill of Robert Gamble for not listening to my friend. But it is my belief that our world would be a nicer place if children would mind their parents and husbands their wives.

THE CHEATER

ROY BAUSCHATZ

MY NAME IS AUGUST JACOB. I am a cabinetmaker by choice, a coffin maker by necessity. I can deal with a man no matter on which side of the hereafter he might find himself.

Building coffins has put me in contact with quite an array of customers. There are the bereaved, of course; family members mourning the loss of a loved one or friends saying good-bye to a mate. Then there are the criminals who have met a bad end and have no one left to grieve their passing. With the British soldiers in town, business is good, since they spread the pox wherever they go. Yes, my clientele is quite varied, but, to be honest, most of them fade from my memory rather quickly. However, there is one dead man I shall never forget.

My tale begins with the arrival in the city of my Uncle Christian, a resident of Philadelphia. Christian is a carter there. He hauls iron, ore, coal, and firewood to the forges. Loading and unloading such cargo has given Uncle Christian huge shoulders and muscular arms, but he is, at heart, a gentle and honest man. My uncle was in town to buy a new wagon and harness for his business. He had ordered the harness some time before, but it was still two days away from completion when he got to town.

Now, as I said, Uncle Christian is a fine man, but he does have a weakness for card games, 'specially if he thinks Aunt Sarah won't find out about it. Now here he was with two days in a city full of boisterous taverns. Uncle Christian visited a few of the taverns until he found a game with an empty chair. He took a seat and laid his wagon and harness money on the table.

My uncle was seated next to a man from Gloucester named Richard Parsons. This fellow was from a good family, but he appeared to have fallen on hard times of late. His skin looked like he was afraid of the light of day, and his clothes were long overdue for a wash. Parsons was a small man who only came to my uncle's shoulder, but he attempted to make up for this with loud talk and constant bragging.

Uncle Christian was very uncomfortable being around Parsons, but a game was a game. As the night progressed, my uncle became convinced that Parsons was not always dealing from the top of the deck. Christian had lost much of his wagon and harness money and was fuming. The more Parsons drank, the sloppier he became and, before long, my uncle caught him blatantly cheating. Christian seized the little man by the front of the shirt and lifted him up so high his toes were barely touching the floor. Looking Parsons right in the eye, my uncle said he would stand for no more cheatin' at this table.

Mr. Parsons got the message and, after Christian shoved him back in his chair, quickly agreed to a new deck of cards and a new game. Soon, my uncle began to win and eventually won back all of his money and then some. True to his name, Christian kept only what was his and gave back some of the money the other players had lost to Parson's cheating.

Parsons had trouble keeping his mouth shut and mumbled and grumbled as his pot of money began to dwindle. He lost hand after hand until he was down to his last shilling. "If I don't win the next hand," he said, "I wish my flesh would fall off and my eyes never shut."

Uncle Christian dealt another hand of cards and, sure enough, Parsons lost. Parsons stumbled off to his bed upstairs in the tavern. Once in his room, he tossed his waistcoat across a chair and his breeches to the floor. As he sat down on the bed to remove his stockings, he noticed a black spot beginning to grow on his leg. Blurry-eyed, he attributed the malady to Christian's manhandling and thought no more of it. In only a minute or two, Parsons was under the sheets and sleeping soundly.

By mid-morning, the innkeeper was concerned that the guest upstairs had not yet come down to break his fast with the others. The man went up the stairs and knocked on the door. There was no answer, but the door was slightly ajar, and a horrible odor came from deep within the room. That's when they called for me.

When I got to the tavern, I saw my Uncle Christian, and he relayed the events of the previous evening.

Now, I have been in the coffin trade for many years, but I was unprepared for what I was about to see. When I pulled back the sheets, flesh fell from the man's bones like melting lard. The victim's eyes were as wide as saucers and locked in a blank stare. It was a delicate operation, but I finally got Mr. Parson's body, or what was left of it, back to my shop.

Using all of my skills, I prepared the dead man as best I could for his final resting place. It took some doing. As I stood back to admire my work, I realized I had not closed his eyes. I took two fingers and pulled them shut. Then I stepped back to look. The dead man's eyes were wide open and seemed to be staring right back at me!

I retrieved two heavy coins, pulled the eyelids shut, and placed the coins on the lids to keep them closed. Before I could turn halfway around, the coins clanked to the floor and the man's eyes were open again.

I removed a needle and thread from my reticule, and I proceeded to sew Mr. Parson's eyes shut. As I walked across the room to return my reticule to its proper place, the stitches on the man's eyes began to pop. Again, the dead man's eyes were open and glaring straight ahead!

I gave some thought to the situation and decided that, given the life Richard Parsons had recently led, he might like to see where he was going in the hereafter. I turned him over and nailed the coffin shut.

This I tell you, good people: Choose your words wisely, for they may foretell your future.

IN THE RIGGING

JOHN P. HUNTER

I RARELY HAVE AN INTEREST in the personal lives of my servants. My footman, Charles, was an exception and not just because he, unlike most in Virginia, was not a slave but had come from England.

There was something special I noticed about the seventeen-year-old Charles from the moment he arrived looking for work. Now, I have a rigorous set of criteria for my servants, and although I most certainly do not bother with the preliminary selections, no one works in my household without my personal approval.

It goes without saying that I am immune to the crassness of mere physical attractiveness, but I cannot deny that I was taken aback by Charles's appearance. I have never seen such crystal-clear blue eyes. His hair was like fine corn silk, and, most startling of all, his teeth were straight and white as fresh cotton. When the boy walked into my parlor, he smiled, which was an affront to my dignity, but I am embarrassed to admit I smiled back at him. This is the effect

Charles had on people.

Charles did a fine job as my footman. He was slight of build and not blessed with great physical strength, attributes that might have disqualified him for my service had my alternatives been as many as in England. Still, he tended my needs in a most efficient and charming way. I should not admit to this, but I actually looked forward to the boy's beautiful smile and cheerful countenance every morning. My breeding would not allow me to get chatty with Charles, but my dear friend Mr. Logan struck up a friendship with the boy.

Occasionally, I would see the two of them leaning against a fence talking. Mr. Logan reported that the lad's fondest ambition was to sail the seas. It was from Mr. Logan that I learned what happened when Charles set off to see the world.

After a year as my footman, Charles had accumulated a small bag of coins. Enough, evidently, to start him on his way to the far corners of the earth. He left his bed of straw in the stables in the middle of the night and vanished into the dark without so much as a fare-thee-well to anyone. I could not bring myself to put a notice for his return in the newspaper.

Charles traveled all the way to the docks at Portsmouth. Undoubtedly using his charm, he soon landed a job on a ship bound for the West Indies. Having such a thin, light frame had its advantages in some shipboard tasks, and Charles found himself high in the rigging, preparing the lines, canvas, and runners for the vessel's imminent departure.

On the morning the ship was to set sail, Charles hung on rigging high up by the tallest mast. He was guiding the pulleys and canvas when a sudden wind gust broke his grip and sent him tumbling headfirst toward the deck. Luckily, he banged against a metal hook on the way down, which lodged securely into his trousers. That slowed him enough to grab a line. Unluckily, the hook pulled Charles's trousers all the way down and over his feet. Tangled in the lifesaving line, he now hung naked from the waist down.

"Well, blast me flat!" a sailor down on deck hollered out. "That man's a woman!"

And so he was. He— "she" I suppose is now the more correct—was given a mangy wrap and immediately dismissed from the ship as women are not allowed to be sailors.

Mr. Logan, who was in Portsmouth on business and witnessed the spectacle, took his friend by the arm and led her away.

Head in hands, she told him, "I cannot live as a woman and be doomed to a life of washing, cleaning, sewing, and raising the children of some doltish husband. If I can't go see the world, I would rather take my own life."

So the generous Mr. Logan bought "Charles" a new pair of sturdy trousers and a strong belt. They then made their way down over to Norfolk, whose residents had not yet heard the tale of the girl in the rigging, and Mr. Logan persuaded a captain to give his friend a job on a ship.

"The last time I saw Charles," Mr. Logan told me on his return, "she was waving at me from high in the rigging."

There was no further word of my former footman until years later when Mr. Logan returned from another trip.

"Well," he reported, "while standing by the docks, a small but fine merchant ship weighed anchor and glided right past my eyes. The sun broke through and illuminated the face of the ship's captain who stood at the helm. He had crystal-blue eyes that sparkled, hair like fine corn silk, and teeth as straight and white as fresh cotton."

PERILS
OF CONSCIENCE

ROY BAUSCHATZ

I GUESS YOU COME TO TOWN for the hangin' just like me. I got me a new waistcoat and a fresh haircut and shave, so's I'd more fit in with the fine gentlemen you see in the city. 'Course when you seen the things I seen and been the places I been, 'taint easy comin' here mix'n with all these fine gentlemen, 'specially lookin' like a merchant sailor.

It's time to follow the rules now tho' I been told. Understand, we had rules on the ship, just different from them ashore. Don't seem easy to follow the ones set up by the magistrate here or the ones the Cap'n called for on the ship. Sometimes the way the Cap'n treats his people, they jus' get fed up . . . like them three that caused this here hangin'.

Seems the three of 'em jumped ship when they last tied up in Baltimore, just run off into the wilderness. That was near three years ago now. Weren't 'til just this spring things started to go astray.

They was just as close as any three shipmates was goin'

to be for the most part, 'les one was gonna' cause the others to be worse off than him. Then it got to be each one to lookin' out fer hisself. Yeah, it's said the three of 'em seen some good times and some bad times. Ole Peter Heckie. Matthew O'Conner, and Bryan Conner, by name. None seemed to care they looked like merchant sailors or even a bit like pirates.

Peter, he was the meanest. Bryan, he just kinda' followed along and did what the others said. Matthew, it's said, he's going by different rules now. It weren't long back tho' that Matthew was happiest when he was stealin' or fightin' or drinkin' more'n his share o' rum. That Matthew sorta' fancied hisself a gentleman. Even without a fresh haircut and a shave, he thought himself to be the best lookin' of the bunch. I been readin' 'bout 'em here in the *Gazette*.

There's a talk in the piece 'bout a William Marr who's a runaway too. Ran from Colonel Chisell up in Hanover County. Been said that the colonel was a hard man to be around—come from his soldier'n days. January last, Marr got fed up just like them sailors. Didn't care his indenture weren't paid, just ran off into the wilderness. Same place as them three shipmates. Marr joined up with them being they was all runnin' from something. Guess he didn't like being in the wilderness by hisself.

They were all short of sumpin' to eat and in need of a warm bed when they came across a leatherstockin' name of Liselet Larby. Had a cabin up in Orange County deep in the wilderness itself. Ole Liselet, bein' a loner, was glad for the company. That night, he treated them all decent with what he had for food and blankets. It was then Liselet let it be known he was headed to the settlement next morning to sell his trappin's and take in some fresh powder and shot.

Peter got the notion Liselet might get to talkin' and

might let it be known in the settlement he had company, revealin' where the runaways got to. That wouldn't do for none of this pack. Peter got the others thinkin', includin' Marr, that they had to do sumpin'. So, Peter made a plan, not knowin' Marr didn't have the same understandin' as them three sailors.

The next mornin', them five new friends set out together for the settlement. Liselet had both arms loaded with his trappin's and no free hand for his musket. Peter, actin' like the helpful sort, reached out to carry it for him.

They got no more'n a couple hundred yard from the cabin when Peter raised the musket and took dead aim at the leatherstocking. BAM! . . . shot him square in the back. Them hides kept the shot from bein' the end for Larby. Peter took notice of this and took to beatin' what life was left outa' Larby with his own musket.

Marr had no stomach for this, but he kept back for fear the three shipmates would turn on him. Weren't long before the sight of Larby layin' there all bloody and wide-eyed took over Marr and he stole off on his own at the first chance there was to free hisself from that pack.

Sleep wouldn't come to Marr, neither could he keep food down nor shake that lifeless apparition always starin' back at'm. Thinkin' it the only way out of these circumstances, he took hisself to the magistrate in Hanover County and was soon givin' an account of all the facts as he knowed 'em. Says what he said right here in the paper.

I been told the newspapers are talkin' about it from Boston to Philadelphia. Can't say for sure who gave the order, but I do know that two men with good horses set off to find Peter and Matthew and Bryan. Only brought back Peter and Bryan. Both stood trial and them bein' the ones this hangin's all about. Seems after the trial, Marr walked free from the courtroom after turnin' king's evidence. Hasn't been seen since.

Makes a person wonder if he's at peace with his soul, talkin' bout his mates like that. Sure would like to know where he's gone and who he's been talkin' to.

Well, I'm off to help swell the crowds at the gallows. Don't want to be too close up, you see, just near enough to see justice is done with me own eyes and see there's no loose ends about talkin' to the sheriff.

And if you see someone about the city calls himself William Marr, tell 'em his ole friend Matthew's lookin' for 'em. Needs to tie up some loose ends.

DISMAL SWAMP

GENE MITCHELL

MY MISTRESS, CATHERINE DRURY by name, is a strong woman. When old massa up and died, she took to running that plantation all by herself. Runs it like a man she does. I should know . . . I'm her maidservant, and I always go where my mistress goes.

We're from Isle of Wight County, near a place called Chandler's Swamp. Mean place, that Chandler's Swamp. Dark and gloomy 'cause them trees are so tall they shut out the sunlight. People say strange and spooky things happen in Chandler's Swamp, but I thought such talk was foolishness. Well, that's what I used to think.

It all started a little while ago when my mistress went down to the courthouse like she does once a month to take care of her affairs. She gets Toby, the stable boy, to hitch up old Caesar to the riding chair, and off we go. I always go where my mistress goes. On the way to the courthouse, there is a low place in the road where it cuts through the swamp. Every time old Caesar gets to that low place, he stops *dead* in his tracks.

Some folks say horses don't have good sense. I say, horses see things that folks can't see. Why, old man Drury would have taken a whip to that poor animal 'cause that's the kind of man he was, but not my mistress. No, she's fond of her horses. So, I would climb down from the chair, grab old Caesar by the reins, walk him down the road a bit, climb back into the chair, and off we'd go.

On the day I'm discussing, mistress was down at the courthouse talking with some of her lady friends. She talked and talked and stayed and stayed. It was nigh on five of the clock when we started for home. Mind you, mistress ain't ever been one to be afraid of the dark, so we were taking our time.

Sure enough, when old Caesar got to that low place he stopped dead right there in his tracks. I was a-fixing to get out of the chair when we saw this light. It come out of the swamp, crossed the road, and went back into the swamp. Then, the light reappeared and seemed to be dancin' around some old logs and limbs all tied together like a raft maybe. And on the raft we saw two figures, a man and a woman. What was so peculiar about it all was that the raft wasn't on the water. It was above the water, and it was coming directly toward us!

That was enough for old Caesar and he *took* off running. That old horse didn't stop running until we reached the big house. Lord, have mercy. We were a sight to be seen . . . old Caesar covered with lather and me and mistress covered with mud.

I yelled to Toby to come quick to help me with mistress. The poor woman had turned white as a sheet, and her hands were cold as ice. She was mumbling something to herself that Toby and me didn't understand. So we got her inside the house. I put her to bed and made her a cup of chamomile tea to calm her down some. She fell into a deep sleep, but, I swear, she had the look of death upon her face.

Later that evening, I walked down to the quarter to talk with ole Moses. I told him what I had seen. He said that be Miss Anne and Massa Robert.

You see, seems like Miss Anne lived on a plantation next to ours. She fell deeply in love with Massa Robert, my mistress's younger brother, and he was crazy in love with Miss Anne. But the young lady's mama and papa had picked out a richer man for their daughter to marry. So Massa Robert decided he'd go away, find his own fortune, and return to ask for Miss Anne's hand in marriage.

While Massa Robert was away, Miss Anne took sick with the swamp fever. That sickness is not a pretty sight. First, you get mighty thirsty . . . there ain't enough water in the world to quench your thirst. Then your skin turns the color of brown swamp water, and the worst of it starts to happen. Flesh starts to falling off your bones, piece by piece and bit by bit. From what they say, it's about the worst pain a body can endure although, really, ain't no one ever endured it for long. There ain't nothing anyone can do for you. Moses said you could hear that poor child screaming in agony all over the plantation. She screamed out Massa Robert's name 'bout as often as she did the good Lord's, but neither one of 'm helped her much. It was probably a good thing when she finally died and got some rest from the pain.

Massa Robert got back and, sure enough, he had made his fortune. Then he learned that his beloved had passed on, and he went to pieces. The poor boy started ranting and raving about how she wasn't dead; how she just wandered off into the swamp and how he was going to go in there and find her and hide her in the hollow of an old cypress tree to keep her safe. Crazy talk like that.

Massa Robert commenced going deeper and deeper into the swamp, living off swamp berries, drinking swamp water, sleeping on the wet ground. Moses said, on quiet nights, you could even hear him call for her, "Anne, Anne, where are you? Please show yourself to me." But she never did. One night, though, when he was about to fall asleep, he saw a light in the swamp. He yelled out to it, but the light disappeared. Master Robert convinced himself that this was his beloved Anne. So the very next day, he built himself a raft made out of dead tree limbs and fashioned himself a pole. He was determined to catch that light out in the swamp.

Massa Robert sat down beside his raft to wait for the light to return. He didn't have to wait for very long. That very same night he saw it. He climbed aboard his raft, grabbed his pole, and started poling out toward the light. The further that light got away from him, the faster he poled and, once, he could almost reach out and touch it. But the light vanished into thin air about the same time the raft fell apart. Massa Robert slowly sank beneath the water of the swamp and drowned.

To this very day, on dark nights in Chandler's swamp, you can still see those two lovers, Massa Robert and Miss Anne, on that raft, united in death. Well, that's what they always said, but I didn't put no stock in it 'til me and my mistress seen what we seen.

As for my mistress, she was never the same after that night. She wouldn't eat, she couldn't sleep. She caught the swamp fever and died. A few days later, I followed her, 'cause you see . . . where mistress goes, I go.

THE
COMBUSTIBLE
WOMAN

JOHN P. HUNTER

AS AN OFFICER ON HMS *ROVER,* a stout and seaworthy frigate, for over fifteen years, I have heard many things that cannot be explained. Down in the West Indies, I've seen the natives cast spells with the heads of chickens to bring back sight to a blind man. In Portugal, my mates and I heard of a man who could float in the air. There is so much magic and conjuring in Africa that I don't have the years left to describe it all. I must say, however, that the strangest thing I have ever seen took place in a small house in the city of Williamsburg in the British colony of Virginia.

After several months of plying the sugar trade in the West Indies, our captain sailed north to avoid hurricane season, and we put in at Norfolk. I passed up the usual few days of relaxation in port to fulfill a promise to my late mother. Her dear sister, Frances, had sailed for Virginia some years before and no one in the family had seen her in decades. Before my mother died, she asked me to pass on a gold locket to her sister whenever my travels took me to the colonies. Since Williamsburg was only fifty or so miles from Norfolk, I had the opportunity to deliver the locket to the woman whom, by the by, I had never met even though she was my aunt.

Luck was with me and I was able to hire a good horse from a stable near the docks. I arrived in Williamsburg in the late afternoon and inquired at a tavern as to the whereabouts of my aunt. I found her house in short order. The dwelling was small but seemed well kept. A freshly painted fence surrounded a fine garden, and I could see a kitchen, smokehouse, and dovecote around back. It was a narrow structure of two stories with a chimney at each end. I took a breath, walked up to the front door, and knocked.

A shy servant girl opened the door and, after a few minutes, showed me into the parlor where I met my aunt. Frances was in her early sixties, erect of carriage, and dressed quite well. She was also intimidating in her way, and I was nervous until her eyes filled with tears and she said, "Oh, my! I see my beloved sister in your eyes! How I have missed her sweet face these o so many years."

Aunt Frances held out her hand to me, and I crossed the room to take it in my own. As I approached my aunt, I detected a strong odor. The smell was not offensive but was quite noticeable and powerful. There was something familiar about it—peculiar, like sassafras, only . . . of course! The scent was oil of camphor! I had some experience with the medicine's aroma as we had once transported several cases of the substance. Many of the sailors swore that spirit of camphor could cure a myriad of ills and prevent others, but I had never sampled it myself.

"What a dashing young officer!" Aunt Frances exclaimed as she took my hand. "Please, my boy, join me for tea."

The evening was enjoyable, and I liked my aunt immediately. She was witty and bright, a most gracious and comfortable hostess. The locket from my mother, her sister, brought more tears, but also led her into some charming tales of their childhood. The early evening passed quickly and pleasantly, and then my aunt asked to be excused for half an hour for "her treatment." She saw the concern on my face and said, "Not to worry, dear nephew. I'm as fit as a fiddle, and for that I credit fully my spirit of camphor treatments."

It seems that for some years and twice a day, Aunt Frances has covered herself from head to toe with spirit of camphor. Once in the morning and once in the evening was her routine, and nothing kept her from it. "Oh, but that everyone would adopt the same regimen," she said. "Why, there would be no more sickness at all."

The exercise certainly seemed to work for my robust aunt, and who can argue with such proof? Frances and her servant girl went upstairs for the treatment, and I busied myself with a *Virginia Gazette* my hostess had thoughtfully provided for my amusement. In less than three quarters of an hour, I was startled by a wave of camphor scent as my aunt came down the stairs. Her skin was glowing with the elixir, and she looked resplendent in a lovely satin dress. I gave some thought to adopting this camphor regimen for myself.

The rest of the evening flew by. Frances was as interested in my travels as I was in her childhood stories about herself and my beloved mother. We shared a small brandy, the hour became late, and Aunt Frances said she needed to retire. She would hear no protest to her offer of a small bedroom on the ground floor for my own use. I settled into the narrow but comfortable bed and was soon sleeping soundly.

In the morning, I was awakened by a shrill scream

from the young servant girl. I rushed into the main room and found the poor girl sobbing in a heap on the stairs. Her only response to my queries was to point a trembling finger up the steps. I bounded up the staircase and into Frances's chamber. I stopped in my tracks, and my hand went involuntarily to my throat in horror. My Aunt Frances was near her bed . . . *burnt to ashes* except for her shinbones, feet, and three fingers of one hand!

After recovering from my shock, I summoned a constable and a tradesman whose duties included preparing the dead for burial. None of the three of us had ever seen anything like the scene in my aunt's bedchamber. The ashes were clammy and stunk intolerably. The walls of the room, the bed, and other furniture were covered with a fine but moist dust. The ceiling was almost covered with a sort of moistness of a yellow color that gave a very offensive smell. Those parts of the body that remained were burned black, but nothing else in the room was consumed.

Common fire would have taken hold of the beds, the chamber, the whole house, but none of that was burned. Besides, there was neither fire nor light in the chamber. The serenity of the air left no room to suspect that lightning was the culprit.

"Has been me sad duty to prepare and inter near a thousand of the dead," said the tradesman, "yet, never have me eyes seen a thing such as this. Best I get what remains of the woman in a box and into the ground forthwith."

"No!" I exclaimed too loudly, for I was not prepared to lose my newfound aunt without knowing more. "Thank you for your kind attention, gentlemen," I said to the constable and tradesman as I calmed down, "but I will handle this myself in appropriate time. Good day."

The men left, and it was a few minutes before I was

in a state to make a rational plan. I dispatched a servant to Norfolk to fetch Dr. Harland, ship's physician—a friend and the most learned man I know. Within a day, the good doctor had arrived at the house. He spent several uninterrupted hours in my aunt's chamber, inspecting, before he emerged with an answer for me. "Your aunt, dear friend, was consumed by a fire that kindled in her own body," he said. "The flame started deep in the veins and the body was consumed in a moment. Your aunt did not suffer even a second of pain."

"How could that be?" I exclaimed.

"That I do not know," the doctor responded. "The body is a complex thing, and we may never understand all of its mysteries. What results in robust health for one may make another deathly ill. Did your aunt perhaps overindulge in any way? Alcohol, a certain herb, too much sunshine, anything at all?"

"Certainly not," I responded. I saw no need to paint her as an odd woman. I wanted her reputation to rest in peace.

I, however, have most certainly not adopted my late aunt's regimen. A year or so later, however, I heard of a ship in Barbados that spontaneously burst into flame in high seas during a driving rain. Its cargo was camphor.

MARRIAGE PLANS

ROY BAUSCHATZ

THIS PROSPEROUS COLONY PROVIDES a cabinet-maker such as myself many opportunities. My business is successful, and I have many loyal customers. However, the busy pace of my early years here did little for my social life. Bachelorhood has certain advantages, and I was reasonably content with my lot in life until I met Lady Mary. She's a most handsome woman and appears to be quite well practiced in the social graces. I can honestly report that I am quite in love with her, though our courtship has not been without some mystery.

Early in our acquaintance, Lady Mary appeared hesitant to share any of her past. Any mention of her younger years prompted her immediately to change the subject. Wags spread word that her father and brothers committed murder before coming here to the colonies. I try to dismiss gossip, but, still, it was troubling. Especially since Lady Mary never denied the talk she must have heard in one way or the other.

I believe there may be some substance in the old

saying, "Marry me, marry my family." Nonetheless, I had deep feelings for Lady Mary and worked hard to gain her trust. Finally, my efforts were rewarded, and she took me into her confidence. She explained a crisis from her past, more than twenty years ago in England.

As handsome as she is today, she was undoubtedly a beauty in her early years. Many suitors flocked around vying for her attention. She chose the brave, gallant, and rich Mr. Fox. No one, including Lady Mary, knew much about Mr. Fox. This only added to Mr. Fox's allure, as did his descriptions of the beautiful castle he said would be their new home.

Any time she asked Mr. Fox about the whereabouts of their new home, he would happily describe where it was, but never did he speak of it to her brothers or father. Lady Mary was aware that even gentlemen will occasionally embellish the truth, especially when it comes to courtship. She was curious about the castle and wanted to see it for herself. After all, she intended to spend the rest of her life there.

A few days before the marriage contract was to be drawn, Mr. Fox was away from town on business, as he described it, and Lady Mary set out on horseback to find the castle. Following the path Mr. Fox had described, she went over seven hills, through seven valleys, and across seven streams. Lady Mary crested the last hill and in the meadow below saw the most beautiful castle she'd ever seen. It was a fine, strong house with thick, high walls and a deep moat.

As Lady Mary crossed the meadow and approached the drawbridge, she saw a sign across the gate that read, "*BE BOLD, BE BOLD.*" Being of strong resolve, Lady Mary did just that. She hid her horse and boldly walked cross the drawbridge and through the gate. Inside the castle, she came upon a doorway with an inscription that read, "*BE*

BOLD, BE BOLD, BUT NOT TOO BOLD." With that, she began to hesitate, but her curiosity was still not satisfied, and she walked deeper into the castle. As she went down a hallway toward a gallery, she came to door with another warning inscribed, *"BE BOLD, BE BOLD, BUT NOT TOO BOLD, LEST YOUR HEART'S BLOOD RUN COLD."*

Have I told you that Lady Mary is a woman of strong resolve? Well, some would call it bravery; others might say it was plain foolishness for a woman, alone with no protection, to proceed further. Lady Mary took a deep breath, put her hand on the door latch, and pushed the door full open. What did she find? Bodies of beautiful young women stacked high upon the floor, their hair and gowns all stained with blood!

Lady Mary quickly turned to flee this horrid chamber. She dashed through the gallery, down the staircase, and into the hall where she looked out the window. Her heart leapt up into her throat. Mr. Fox was dragging another beautiful young lady across the drawbridge and through the gate.

Lady Mary hid herself behind a large cask near the entry. Mr. Fox dragged in the young girl who had fainted dead away. Mr. Fox spotted a diamond ring on the unconscious girl's finger. Try as he would, he could not pull the ring free. So he pulled out his knife and brought it down on the young woman's finger.

The blow caused the finger to fly up in the air and land squarely in Lady Mary's lap. Mr. Fox looked everywhere for the ring. Lady Mary closed her eyes and tried to breathe as slowly and silently as she could as he approached the cask. At that moment, the young girl let out a scream. Abandoning his search, Mr. Fox dragged the young lady upstairs to the bloody chamber.

As soon as Mr. Fox passed out of sight, Lady Mary ran

out of the castle, across the drawbridge, and to her hidden horse. She galloped across the seven streams, valleys, and hills until she was safely back home.

The very next day, Lady Mary and Mr. Fox were to sign the marriage contract over breakfast at her father's country home. As they sat down to breakfast, Mr. Fox was seated across the table from Lady Mary who sat next to her father. Her brothers were on either side of Mr. Fox.

Mr. Fox observed that Lady Mary appeared to be quite pale and inquired if she was well. She explained that she had not slept well last night and told them all she'd had horrible dreams.

Mr. Fox said that dreams are often the contrary of reality but asked her to tell them of the dream so they could determine for themselves. He suggested that her sweet voice would make the time pass quickly, and all would be happy 'til the marriage hour came.

Lady Mary recounted the events of the last day as though it was surreal. "I dreamed that I found your castle with the strong, high walls and large moat in a meadow many hours from here. As I crossed the meadow and approached the drawbridge, I saw a sign across the gate that read, '*BE BOLD. BE BOLD.*'"

Mr. Fox said, "It is not so, nor was it so."

"And when I came upon the doorway," Lady Mary continued, "across the doorway I found an inscription that read, '*BE BOLD, BE BOLD, BUT NOT TOO BOLD.*'"

Mr. Fox looked a little uncomfortable but repeated, "It is not so, nor was it so."

"Ah! But then I saw another sign that read, '*BE BOLD, BE BOLD, BUT NOT TOO BOLD, LEST YOUR HEART'S BLOOD RUN COLD.*' I opened the door and saw bodies and skeletons of beautiful, young women stacked high upon the floor!" Lady Mary said, trembling at the memory. "Their hair and gowns were all stained with blood!"

Mr. Fox trembled once himself and said, "It is not so, nor was it so. And God forbid it should be so."

"Then I dreamed that I rushed down near the entry just in time to hide myself behind a cask as you dragged a beautiful young lady through the gate. As you passed me, you saw a diamond ring on the girl's finger," Lady Mary said, near tears. "Try as you might, you could not pull the ring free, so you pulled out your knife and cut off young girl's finger to get the diamond!"

Mr. Fox said *very* nervously, "It is not so, nor was it so. And God forbid it should be so." Mr. Fox rose from his seat as though to say something else, but Lady Mary said, "But it is so, and it was so. Here's the finger and the ring I have to show."

With that, she held out the poor young woman's finger, still wearing the ring, and pointed it directly at Mr. Fox.

Mr. Fox tried to leap up and run for the door, but Lady Mary's father and brothers were too fast for him. They drew their swords and cut him to pieces.

So you see, I am faced with a dilemma. On one hand, if I marry Lady Mary, I get her father and brothers in the bargain, and I can ill afford to anger them. On the other hand, Lady Mary is *such* a handsome and gracious woman.

DROWNING IN FASHION

JOHN P. HUNTER

HENRY, JOHN, AND HUGH WERE handsome, carefree, daring and, as the twenty-year-old sons of wealth, gentlemen with too much time and money on their hands. They were not malicious by nature even though some of their antics did at times disrupt the peace. They would race their fine horses down the middle of the main street, lead boisterous songs late at night, gamble on anything, and generally cause much worry in the community.

More than one citizen had attributed the young men's boundless energy to the absence of wives. There were some enthusiastic flirtations with tradesmen's daughters and the occasional country girl, but there were no acceptable marriage prospects on the horizon. Then the Hanover sisters came to Virginia.

Mary, Rachel, and Abigail accompanied their mother to her sister's plantation for a round of visiting. The big house and fields were impressive to most and easily the largest property in the area. But to sisters accustomed to the golden drawing rooms of London and Paris, all this looked like a forsaken wilderness.

In less than half a day, everyone, including John, Hugh, and Henry, knew the three pretty sisters were in the area. There were proper ways for young people to be introduced, of course. The young men's parents, eager for their sons to settle down, conspired with the aunt of the sisters, and soon a dinner was arranged. Nothing so far in their lives had prepared the young gents for the Hanover sisters.

Even though Henry, Hugh, and John wore their finest clothes, they felt like chimney sweeps when the girls made their grand entrance. The three Hanovers were resplendent in French silk and lace, glittering jewels, powdered faces, red lips, and hair piled fashionably—and mountain-high—on their heads. The young men were struck dumb.

Abigail, Mary, and Rachel could easily see the effect they were having on the men and took full advantage. After the sophisticated dandies who had buzzed around them in Paris, these country bumpkins were hardly a challenge. They threw out French bon mots, made condescending remarks, and generally tortured the boys unmercifully. By the time the servants had cleared the table, the three young gentlemen were thoroughly beaten.

Unwilling to end the fun, Rachel suggested they all walk through the garden and then take a ride in a boat her aunt kept by the river. "Unless," she said in a snooty way, "you *gentlemen* have farm chores to attend to."

"We are at your service," stammered Hugh.

"I know," Rachel said.

Mary offered that she could not possibly stray that far from the house without a footman. Abigail and Rachel agreed, so each took a footman.

There were two boats at the dock. The first was a wide,

comfortable craft with padded seats. It took the Hanover sisters fully ten minutes to arrange themselves, with their servants' help. Every ruffle of their French silk had to be just so, but at last they were ready. The boys took positions at the oars and the servants pushed the boat away from shore. Then the three servants got into small rowboat and trailed a few yards behind, in case the ladies needed something.

The large boat was heavy and the rowing required some exertion. "My, my," Mary sniffed, "I don't recall ever seeing three gentlemen perspire quite so much."

"I don't recall ever seeing a *true* gentleman perspire at *all*," Abigail added.

It was then that the bow of the boat hit a submerged log and overturned. There were screams, much splashing, and a great flailing of arms as the servants rowed quickly into the melee. After a panicked and confusing minute, Abigail and Rachel were on the servants' boat and Henry, Hugh, and John were hanging on to their overturned craft.

"Where is Mary?!" Rachel screamed out. "Oh, dear Lord! My sister is drowned!"

One of the footmen, a big man named Samuel, dived off the boat and disappeared into the water. As a younger man, Samuel had learned to swim and it was a good thing as no one else in the tragedy could swim a lick. Samuel swam down about ten feet and then he saw her. Mary's fine silk and crinolines had absorbed so much water that they held the poor girl on the river bottom like an anchor!

Samuel grabbed Mary's hair in his teeth and pulled up toward the surface with powerful strokes. Just as they broke the surface, Mary's wig came off in Samuel's teeth, and down she went again!

Only a few feet down, Samuel caught up to Mary, grabbed the back of her dress, and pulled her up to safety.

The terrified girl coughed up water, gagged, and swooned, but she would recover. They all made it to shore and dragged up onto the lawn. Drenched from head to toe with their finery in tatters, powder running down their cheeks, and wigs somewhere out in the river, the sisters did not look quite so intimidating.

John began to chuckle. Henry fought it but soon joined in. Hugh started laughing, and, in moments, the three gents were howling with unrestrained laughter. Mortified, the three sisters gathered up their soaking skirts as best they could and ran weeping across the garden and into the house.

"Well," Henry said. "I suppose those who sacrifice to French fashion either go astray or straight to the bottom."

DEADLY ERROR

JOHN P. HUNTER

ALTHOUGH ONE AND ALL HAVE TOLD ME the horrible tragedy was not of my making, I still hear the screams and moans. They will never leave my mind.

In 1776, I was a nurse in the employ of the McGregor family in Charlestown, near Boston. It was my understanding that Mr. McGregor's brothers, sisters, and parents remained in Scotland, and only he had struck out for the new world where he had made quite a nice life for himself. Mr. McGregor was a fervent patriot in the American cause, but a stubborn infection had curtailed his activities and put him flat in the bed. When I first arrived, the poor man was burning up with fever. I knew some tricks and treatment and soon had him resting more comfortably. Mrs. McGregor was most grateful for my efforts and proved to be a very kind woman if somewhat nervous and high strung. They had a pretty little daughter of about five named Bonnie who often sang to her father. Mr. McGregor had weathered the worst and would soon be back on his feet. Or so we all hoped.

An almost constant stream of wild-eyed riders and frantic travelers spun stories of the battles at Lexington and Concord and, now, a furious conflict at Bunker Hill that was so very near us. We heard of redcoats killing every man, woman, and child they encountered. Many evacuated our town, but we could not safely transport Mr. McGregor.

The sound of musket fire could soon be heard nearby. A neighbor rushed in and said the British had set the town on fire, and the fire was out of control. Bonnie grabbed for her mother. Clutching each other for dear life, they sobbed and sank down to the floor. "Pray, Bonnie, pray!" Mrs. Mc-Gregor wailed.

There was smoke in the hallway as I rushed to check on Mr. McGregor. As I entered his room, the man was coughing violently from the smoke, and I could see that end of the house was indeed on fire.

He was very weak and woozy, and his full weight almost dropped us both to the floor. At that moment, I heard terrified screams from Bonnie and her mother!

"Spare us!" I heard Mrs. McGregor scream, presumably at some British soldier. "God help us!"

This was too much for Mr. McGregor. Some internal strength came over his weakened body, and he broke away from me, grabbed his sword next to the door, and ran through the smoke toward his family.

When I made it to the main room, I witnessed a horrible sight. Mrs. McGregor, out of her mind with fear, laying in a ball. Little Bonnie ran around in a frenzy. Flames ran down the hallway and licked up the walls.

But the look on Mr. McGregor's face was the worst thing of all. He looked down at a dead British soldier. Mr. McGregor had run him through from front to back with his sword, but there was no look of triumph on the husband and father's face. As he stared into the open eyes of the dead redcoat, he spoke in a tortured voice, "I have killed my brother!"

His torture did not last long. In a panic myself, I rushed through the door and out into the street yelling for help. Only a second or two later, the entire house was in flames, and the heavy, flaming roof caved in, killing all inside.

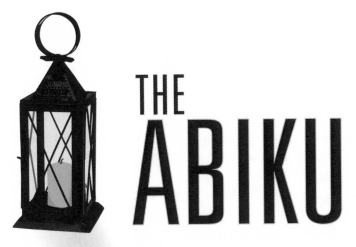

THE ABIKU

GENE MITCHELL

MY PAPA COME ALL THE WAY TO VIRGINIA on a slave ship. Before I was sold off, my papa used to sit me on his knee and tell me how *his* mama and papa come to be!

When papa was a boy, there lived in his village an old Abiku, which is an evil one who cast spells on folks—a night witch, some say. This old man had a very pretty daughter named Zera. She was so beautiful that she had more sweethearts than a man has fingers and toes. Her papa didn't like any of them. Still they kept on coming round and pestering his household.

Truth be known, the papa didn't want her to marry because she had magical powers of her own that the old man did not want shared. By 'n by, he sent word far and wide that any man who cleared six acres of land, rolled up the logs, and piled up the brush in one day—that man could jump the broom with his daughter. That's 'bout as easy as climbing a greased pole with two baskets of eggs! Well, all them young men just dropped by the wayside except for one named Amari.

Amari was a strapping and handsome fellow who looked strong enough to knock a bull down. He loved Zera something fierce, and she loved him back. One day, Amari got up the nerve to speak with the old man. This was not an easy thing to do, for Zera's papa was as ugly as Zera was beautiful. His skin was like leather, and he was blind in one eye. He walked bent over with a gnarled stick to help him on his way. When he spoke, he had a high-pitched, squeaky voice.

"Good morning, sir," Amari said. "I hear that you have work to do here, and I came to see if I could do this wonderful thing and win your beautiful daughter."

The old man crooked his head to one side and said, "Fine by me. You start in the morning."

Amari wanted to start right then, and he wondered why he had to wait until the morning. But the Abiku use the night to do their evilness. If an Abiku is mad at you, he comes to your house. He say, "Denda Mar Twan Kano, Denda Mar Twan Kano" ("you will die, you will die!"). You hear someone calling you at nighttime, never, never answer, unless you are certain who it is. He may be outside your door. If you answer, he will catch your life and suck your blood, and you will die. Being that the old man was a night witch, Zera gave Amari a golden ring to keep him safe. Them evil ones don't like shiny things. With that, Amari went off as happy as a jaybird who'd just robbed a sparrow's nest!

Early the next morning, Amari came by the house to get an axe to do the work. Zera ran and got it for him. When no one was looking, she sprinkled black dust upon it and said, "Axe you cut." She gave Amari the axe and a little leather pouch filled with magical shells. She told Amari to shake the little pouch and the axe would do all the work.

Amari went off into the forest. He remembered what Zera had told him and shook the little leather pouch with the shells. The axe flew out of Amari's hands and began to chop down the trees so fast that Amari only saw a cloud of wood chips. The more he shook the little leather pouch, the faster the axe worked. Trees were coming down all over the place, logs were rolling up, and the brush was disappearing like hoecakes at suppertime. Amari could have finished before the sun was high above the trees, but he hung back because he didn't want Zera's papa to know he had done the work through conjuring. He finished the last bit himself. Long before sunset, the whole six acres were cleaned up.

The old Abiku saw what wondrous things Amari had done, and he was mad. He didn't know what to do or what to say. One thing for sure, he was not going to give up his daughter. "Look like you real handy with that axe!" said the old man.

"Yes sir," said Amari, "When I start to working, I won't stop until I gets the work done!"

"Well, since you so spry and all," said the Abiku, "there's two more acres across the creek. Clear those up before the sun leaves the last branch of that tree yonder and you shall have my daughter in marriage."

When the old man was out of sight, Amari shook the little leather pouch with the shells, and the axe flew out of his hands again. Before you could blink an eye, the trees were cut, piled up, and the brush cleared away.

Amari returned to the old Abiku's house to claim his bride, but trouble was a' brewing. The old man was getting as sour as week-old buttermilk. Zera took Amari by the hand and whispered, "We have to leave this place because Papa's fixing to kill you!"

Zera grabbed a hen's egg out of a basket, a meal sack,

and a skillet with one hand and Amari with the other. Then they took off running.

When the old man saw them two running off, he got madder than a wet hen. He snorted like a horse. Blue smoke came out of his nose, and his eyes turned blood red. The Abiku called upon his evil powers. What was once crooked now was straight. What was blind was now clear. He grabbed a big knife and ran after them. Faster than lightning he was.

He had almost caught up with 'em, when Zera yelled to Amari, "Throw down your coat!" The instant the coat hit the ground, a big, thick, dark wood sprang up. The old Abiku just slashed his way through with his big knife and kept on coming. Soon, he caught up with them again. This time Zera dropped the hen's egg upon the ground. When it broke, a dense fog rose up. For a time Zera's papa was lost.

Then he began to pray, "Bagba! Bagba! O God of the fierce wind, blow this fog away!" Just like that, the wind blew, the fog vanished, and the old man kept on coming.

When Zera's papa reached out to grab Amari's shirttail, Zera dropped the meal sack and the mighty river Ogun appeared. Zera's papa was in such a hurry, he tried to drink the river dry. When he could not, he took a deep breath and blew on the water. His breath was as hot as a furnace, and he turned the mighty Ogun into steam. He was soon upon the lovers again.

By this time, things were getting desperate. Zera and Amari were running as fast as they could, but the old Abiku was running faster. Zera dropped the skillet, and darkness covered the land.

"Abonsom, O God of evil, turn this darkness into day," the old man cried. The dark turned into light, and soon he was as close to Zera and Amari as a bark on a tree.

When he was about to grab Amari, Zera shouted to Amari to drop a shell from the little leather pouch. When he did, lo and behold, a hill sprang up, but the old man just climbed over the hill lickety-split. "Drop another shell, Amari." This time a mountain sprang up, but the witch man climbed up one side and down the other.

"Drop the whole bag, Amari," shouted Zera, and when the little pouch hit the ground, a big stone wall sprang up. This time, it was too tall for the Abiku to climb over, too wide for him to go around, and too deep for him to crawl under. Zera's papa tried, he tried, and he tried. He called upon all the gods he knew, but they did not answer. Soon, the spell wore off, and the old man became crippled and blind in one eye again. He returned to his house alone.

You see, if the old man had not been so evil and hard-headed, he would have had his daughter beside him, a son who would help him tend the fields, and grandchildren to bounce upon his knee.

So let this be a lesson to you all . . . if you want to keep love close, you have to let it go!

THE HANGING

JOHN P. HUNTER

THERE ARE SOME MEN WHO DO NOT think the admirable tenets of hard work and honesty apply to them. Anthony Francis Dittond of Spotsylvania County was such a man.

No one is inclined to like a man who treats everyone like a servant, brags loudly about his purported accomplishments, and sniffs with indifference at anything not directly related to himself. A rich gentleman or royal son could successfully navigate through life in this manner, but Dittond had a problem . . . no money. Strutting around like a king loses much of its luster when the clothes are tattered and the stomach empty. Dittond was facing his worst fear and ultimate insult, a job, when he discovered crime.

Anthony Francis Dittond took to crime like a deer to a salt lick. His first foray into the arena was lucrative and oh so simple. A drunken gentleman was weaving between two buildings late at night. Dittond saw an opportunity. He pulled his scarf up over his face, pushed the drunkard to the ground, and simply took the man's money purse.

To Dittond, it was nothing short of supreme justice that a vastly superior man such as himself should enjoy the fruits accumulated by inferior beings. He became quite the accomplished thief in and around the county seat. He robbed drunkards, tradesmen on their way home, travelers in their tavern rooms, and even women on the way to market. He was amazingly adept at using different voices and employing limps, eye patches, wigs, pillows beneath his waistcoat, and a variety of costumes to throw off his victims' recollections.

As welcome as his money was, his treatment of tavern keepers, barmen, and others led to his being banned from several of the most respected establishments. He also ran up high bills with the tailor, boot maker, wig shop, and silversmith, and he ignored court orders that he settle up. All these creditors, accompanied by a constable, descended on Dittond on the same morning. Dittond was incensed. "How dare you?" he shouted. "Don't you know who I am?"

The constable did not care. "Three days," the humorless constable said. "Three days to pay your debts or you will be locked up in the county jail until you pay what you owe."

His creditors and the constable walked away.

"The Devil with them all!" Dittond shouted to his empty room. "And the Devil with this insignificant town! I shall go to New York or Philadelphia where a man of my stature is appreciated!"

Dittond was out of money, and it would be impossible to travel without ready cash. Of course, he knew how to get some. In his haste, Dittond got careless, and that evening's first victim recognized his assailant. The hunt was on. Desperate and with only a few stolen pence in his pocket, Dittond spotted the coach maker, Mr. Evans, locking up his shop. Staying to the shadows, Dittond followed Mr. Evans as he walked his horse out of town and onto the dark road leading to his home. Dittond took a short cut across a field and laid in wait behind a thick oak tree.

As Mr. Evans rode past the tree, he was hit in the back of the head by something heavy and solid. The coach maker tumbled to the ground, hurt badly, but conscious. As he rose to his knees and fumbled for his small pistol . . . *Crash! Crash! Bam! Bam! Bam!* . . . Five vicious blows to his head and face! Mr. Evans slumped over dead.

Dittond dropped his bloody weapon and casually put on Mr. Evans's waistcoat, coat, and hat. Pleased with the amount of money in the dead man's pockets and purse, the murderer mounted Mr. Evan's horse and rode away.

Between the first victim's account and Dittond's abandoned coat at the scene of Mr. Evan's murder, there was no doubt as to the killer's identity. Never had there been such an enthusiastic manhunt. Practically every man with a horse in town leapt into the saddle and rode after Dittond. By dawn, the riders caught up to Dittond and Mr. Evan's exhausted horse.

All the way back to town, the prisoner taunted the men with tales of his cleverness.

"All I want," said the tailor, "is for the man to either show some remorse or, at the very least, shut his mouth."

Dittond did neither.

A few weeks later, he was tried at the General Court in the Capitol at Williamsburg. Even then, he was cocksure and condescending. Addressing the judges—the governor and his councillors no less—Dittond exclaimed: "This court has no right to compare the value of some insignificant coach maker's life to my own!"

The trial was over quickly, and Dittond was sentenced to the gallows. A mile or two out Capitol Landing Road, a large and curious crowd gathered on the day of the hanging. The noose was placed around Dittond's neck. The minister read prayers and encouraged him to repent, but even that did not wipe the sneer from his face. The gate was opened, and the murderer swung from the gallows. By all accounts, Dittond swung by his neck for over three minutes but would not die.

The crowd was speechless as the man flailed and kicked for what seemed like forever. Then the rope broke, and the condemned man fell to the ground. Dittond stood and spoke. "I suppose you can all pray for me now," he said. "After all, I feel sure you will see me again."

Again, the executioner put the noose around Dittond's neck. The gate was opened, Dittond dropped, and the rope snapped his neck. This time he died instantly, though his eyes stayed open, and a sneer stayed fixed on his lips

And that was the end of Anthony Francis Dittond, though it must be noted that there have been a series of unsolved robberies of late.

ICY HELL

JOHN R. HAMANT

THE SUMMER NIGHT WAS HOT, with mist around the lamplights. The Raleigh Tavern, welcoming in daylight, looked somehow forbidding in the dark. When we crossed the threshold, the temperature dropped to an uncomfortable chill. We walked into the dimly lit dining room. Growing accustomed to the light of two small candles, I saw a bent old man in a dark corner of the room, cowering by the wall. He clutched a dirty ragged cloth against his chest.

"What's all this then?" he croaked. "Looks like you been doing some walking.

"You ought not be in here," he went on. "If you failed to notice, the tavern is closed. Ain't nobody on the place but me . . . they all gone off.

"Ain't nobody comin' here neither . . . not on this night. Won't nobody come here on this night 'cause this is the night . . . this is the night the stranger come two year ago.

"Well, that aside," he said as he ran his rag across our table, "I suppose I ought remember my civilities. My name is Bob Hallam, and I ain't no servant neither. I'm a free man with a trade," he said proudly. "Least I had a trade. I was a mate aboard ship in the coastal trade out of Norfolk 'til that storm caught us up. We was dismasted, and my legs and frame got all broke up.

"I couldn't easy follow my trade no more," he said. "My wife, God rest her, she were dead. No children and no place to go. It were Mrs. Southall, wife of the gentleman what owns this tavern, who said I should come up here to Williamsburg. I told her straight out that I would only come if I could be of use, and that's what I am . . . of use."

He brightened a bit. "I keep the accounts, make certain that the goods that are ordered come proper, and I clean about as I am able to do. But only at night, or when nobody is about, for I don't take kindly to strangers no more . . . not after two year ago."

The old man stopped. Face etched with an inner struggle, he limped painfully toward the window. "I been thinking . . . perhaps the time in my life has come that I should tell someone what happened that night."

We waited.

"It were a night very different from this," he began. "It had been storming off and on all day long, and by nightfall, it were unnaturally cold. About ten of the clock I was out front sweeping off the steps when I looked down the street and seen something I never seen before. It looked like a walking haystack . . . all rounded at the top but with legs and feet like a man. I stood there and watched this thing come toward me, and as it got closer, I could see it were a man. He were all wrapped up in blankets . . . had blankets over his head, over his shoulders, and around his middle . . . like it were the coldest day the world had ever known. He walked up to me at those steps and just stood there and stared. Never said a word.

"I said to him, 'Stranger, there's still a small fire in the dining room hearth if you care to come in and warm yourself.' He didn't say nothing, but when I turned, he followed me in. When he spied that little bit of fire in that hearth, he went right for it. Just stood there staring at those glowing embers like he wanted to walk right into them. Me, I decided to be hospitable, ease him of his burden. I reached up to take the blankets from around his shoulders, and he said, *'DON'T TOUCH ME!'*

"He had a voice that would make your skin crawl, and when he talked, you could see his breath like on a cold winter's day. Well, I backed right off. After a minute or two with him just standin' there, I said, 'well stranger, will you sit?' *'DON'T SIT!'* he said in a voice like from the grave.

"I gathered up my courage and began to ask the stranger questions. He would answer me but with only a few words at a time. That's how I learned his tale . . . and what a tale it were.

"The stranger were a sailor too . . . out of Gloucester, up in the Massachusetts colony. A sailor on the whaling ships. One year when the whales were thin, the captain determined that they were to go way north, further north than they ever been before . . . way past the point of Greenland to the seas where the ice floats around.

"They were up in them seas looking for those whales when they seen a huge mountain of ice floating in the sea. From around behind it, there comes a ship. Well, the captain spied out the ship, and he could see she were most dismasted. What sails there was was all ripped up and blowing in the wind, and she were listed to starboard.

"The captain said they needed to put a boat over and get some men on that ship to see if they could give assistance. So, it were the captain, the stranger, and three of the crew all rowed across. They come around the aft end, where the great cabin windows are and, while the men steadied the boat, the captain stood up in her and peered in them windows. With what little light there was, the captain could see a man sitting at a desk with a pen in his hand. Well, the captain beat on them windows, but that man never moved. So then they come round to the starboard side."

The old man paused, then seemed ready to continue.

"The men climbed onto a deck covered with a foot of undisturbed snow. They dug out the hatchway, went down 'tween decks and straight back to that great cabin and flung open the doors. There that man sat at his desk with his log-book open to its last entry . . . dated sixteen years before! It read, *'Stuck fast in the ice, no food, all dead . . . no hope!'* He was froze. You could see the white of the bone sticking out of his hand and a crack of ice across his eyeball."

We all shivered.

"All them sailors wanted was to get shed of that place. They left the great cabin headed at a fast clip for the topside. Every direction they looked in, there was a froze crewman and another and yet another. The stranger said he commenced to lose his senses with all the horrors presenting themselves to his eyes, and he began to back away. Suddenly, something seized the back of his leg. He turned and looked down and seen the poor froze little cabin boy. He were all crouched down, reaching out just like this."

The old man reached out his hand but quickly drew it back in disgust. "Like he was reaching out for the warmth of the grave.

"The stranger said he lost his senses at that point," the old man said. "He commenced to screaming, and they had to tie him up to get him in the boat and back to the ship. All the way back to Gloucester, he wouldn't eat or drink, and he was always cold. When they got back to Gloucester, they put him off that ship, and that's when he commenced to walking. He always walked south, toward the sun and the warm. For almost two years, that poor man walked as he could from Gloucester, Mass., 'til he showed up at this tavern. Almost two years of everybody shunning him, never once being offered a crumb or roof over his head. He said he done evil things, too, and that if he could no longer find warmth on this earth, he would be sure to find it in the eternal fire down below."

The old man shook his head sadly. "I didn't know what to think. Then it came to me . . . someone should show this poor man a kindness. I said to the stranger, 'I can't offer you much, but the tavern is near empty. There's a small closet above stairs with a small pallet if you would care to go up and take your ease.'

"The stranger stood there staring into that dying fire and said, 'GOD BLESS YOU!' Then he turned and walked ever so slow up them stairs.

"I knew there weren't no sleep for me that night. It occurred to me that maybe I was the first person to show the stranger any kindness since his episode on the charnal ship. It struck me as sad that, even though none of it were his fault, he was all alone without nobody caring for him a whit. Shortly before dawn, as was my custom, I come back in here with my rag to wipe down the tables . . . to make them all clean and shiny for the business of the day."

Then, with the greatest sorrow I ever heard, the old man said, "All of a sudden this drop . . . this little tiny drop hit the back of my hand." Limping back to the corner, he continued, "I looked up, and I could see it come from the ceiling."

We followed his gaze up to the stained spot on the ceiling.

Tight in the corner, bent in terror, the old man went on. "So I crept up them stairs, eased open that closet door, and there the stranger lay on the pallet . . . dead . . . *and melting!* The water coming off him, steam rising off it, steam rising off him. I never seen anything like this before in my life. I went to fetch Dr. Galt. He were a learned man who would know what to do. But by the time we got back, that man were gone. There weren't nothing left but blankets and old clothes and shoes and a puddla' icy water. So the good doctor and I, we threw it all out in the yard and burned it . . . burned it all."

The old man paused and seemed to recover himself somewhat. "Ever since that drop hit the back of my hand," he quickly covered the unmoving hand clutching the dirty rag. "Ever since then, my hand don't work no more, and it's cold like ice. That cold, she done crept up my arm and buried herself deep inside me. I suppose I will have a mind to start walking toward the sun myself before too long."

The old man continued excitedly, "I only tell you this 'cause I commenced to thinking . . . what is the greatest treasure a person can have? Most folks say it's gold, or jewels, or land, but it ain't none of that." Then in a pleading voice, "The greatest treasure a person can have is to be paid a little attention, be remembered . . . by somebody. So, maybe, someday if you read in your newspaper of an occurrence to the south about a man who dies and melts away to nothing . . . maybe you'll give a thought to old Bob and the kindness I've shown you this night."

With a look of embarrassment, the old man returned to the real world. "Well, I'm gonna' show you a kindness now. I'm gonna' turn you out for you ought not be in here on this night, not never on this night!"

The old man then spoke softly. "All of you . . . all of you

. . . you beware of strangers." He turned and started out of the room. "Go along with you now, go on . . . get!"

Then he was gone. Impossibly, the room seemed even colder. All I wanted to do was return to the steamy warmth of the street. We rushed out and drank in the summer air, but it was some time before we could stop shivering.

LOVING
SISTERS

JOHN R. HAMANT

LOOKING FOR ANSWERS ARE YOU? So curious, so needful, so anxious to know what is on the other side of the grave. I could show you, you know, just as I showed *her.* You could then walk hand in hand with us forever.

Oh, I know why you have come. You are no different from so many others. You stink of anticipation. Hoping for a sense, a touch, a glimpse of *her,* the noted Lady Skipwith. Well, you may calm yourselves. She will not come to you, for I shall not permit her presence.

If only you knew how you waste your effort searching for that simpering fool who, it is said, hanged herself for love. It is a tale that has been told for generations, a tale still told by those not bright enough, or brave enough, to tell the real story. Shall I tell you? Do you truly wish to know? Do you hunger to understand the unspeakable power of hatred, resentment, and jealousy? Are you willing to risk madness?

The foolish tale that is told, even today, is of a beautiful girl named Anne who caught the eye of the rich, power-ful, and lustful Sir Peyton Skipwith. They soon were wed, and Anne took up residence at his Eden-like plantation in the western part of the colony. Her life was perfect, and all that she desired was lavished upon her, but her perfect world was soon to crumble.

A grand ball was to be held one evening at the Gover-nor's Palace, a night of music, dancing, beauty, and grace. All of the best families were invited, including Sir Peyton and Lady Anne Skipwith. In keeping with their station, it would be improper for the couple to stay in a tavern, so arrangements were made to lodge as honored guests of Elizabeth and George Wythe.

On the night of the ball, Sir Peyton and Lady Anne made their way to the Governor's Palace. Anne was dressed in her finest. Through minuets and country dances, Sir Peyton and Lady Anne swirled across the ball-room floor admired by all . . . save one. Me. I, her *dear* sister, stood alone in the corner. But what did she know? Certainly not that her dear husband had cast his eye upon me as well, and we had secretly shared our passion before they had been wed.

During a pause in the dancing, Anne went to look for her husband. He had told her that he was going to briefly take the air in the garden, but he had been gone for much too long. Searching the garden, Anne finally came across him, locked in deep embrace . . . with me. Fired with ha-tred and humiliation, Anne ran crying through the ball-room and the hall and out the front door. Crossing the green to the Wythe house, she lost one of her shoes.

Bursting through the front door, she ran up the stair-way, the dull sound of her stockinged foot a counterpoint to the sharp bang of her remaining shoe. She seized a rope that had been used to bind the trunks and tied one end to the landing rail, the other end round her neck, and flung herself over the landing and into eternity.

For years it has been said that the unusual sound of her running feet can be heard in the stillness of the night as she ran to take her own life. So sad, so tragic . . . and such a lie.

True enough, Anne was beautiful, pure, and trusting, beloved by all who knew her. And I, dark and brooding, held a power over men. The events proceeded just as I have told you . . . until the very end.

After Anne burst through the doors and fled up the stairs, her remaining shoe beating out that strange tattoo, she entered her chamber and collapsed on the bed in tears. Some minutes later she heard the sound of someone coming up the stairs. Thinking it was her husband filled with remorse and anxious to beg for forgiveness, she rose and went out to the landing to meet him. But it wasn't her husband. It was me.

As she approached, I could see that her anger had been replaced by something even more horrible. It was there in her eyes, blinding me and burning into my soul—love, forgiveness . . . and PITY! I screamed with rage, grasped her beautiful dress, and flung her down the stairs! I recall how the thud of her body and the crack of her neck sounded so similar to her one-shoed dash up the same stairway.

I returned to the ball and had a delightful evening. After the proper mourning period, I became the new Lady Skipwith. Sir Peyton never questioned what happened. He was as much a fool as Anne was beautiful. The two were ridiculously suited for each other.

Some time later, a few years after my marriage to Sir

Peyton, I came across my late sister's dancing slippers, painstakingly and lovingly preserved *in my husband's old bed trunk!* In a mad rage, I grabbed those slippers and raced down the stairs. Suddenly and soundlessly, Anne's white cat was at my feet. I did not see her until it was too late. I tripped on the cat and tumbled headlong down the stairs. Well, I broke my neck and woke up as a spirit in my own personal hell.

You foolish people. You think that love is the powerful passion. No, it is hate that opens the door to the other side. Hate that guides your ear to that which no one else may hear and your eye to the unseen. Hate is the doorway through which I pass to tease you with the delights of an eternal journey. Listen. Do you hear the sounds, the sounds of the dead? No? A pity. It is obvious you are not ready to join me as yet. But when you are, I shall be waiting, always waiting.

A MOTHER'S LOVE

SHARON ROGERS

THE CRUMBLING STONES in the Bruton Parish Church graveyard carry the names of men and women of note as well as many who were not. Only one is of importance to me. Stand at the west door of the church, face north, and walk thirty-four paces. On your right will be a tomb where you will read:

> Here lies the body of James Whaley
> Of Yorke County in Virginia Who
> Departed this life the 16 day of May
> Anno Domini 1701 and in the fiftieth
> Yeare of his age
> His body lyes to be Consumed to Dust
> Till the Resurrection of the Just
> Amongst which number He'll in hopes appeare
> His blessed Sentence at doomsday to heare.

He was a good man and a good husband. I do not grieve his death, for his life was full. He had lived a fair amount of time—fifty years. But walk around the tomb to the east side. You will read:

> Matthew Whaley lyes Interred here
> Within this Tomb upon his father dear
> Who Departed
> This Life the 26th of
> September 1705 Aged
> Nine years only Child
> of James Whaley
> And Mary his Wife.

This child I grieve with all my heart. Only nine years old. Our only child. Oh, my Mattey, for that is what I called him, Mattey. He was only five years of age when his father departed this life. He was my comfort and my joy. His father knew that he would not live to see Mattey as a grown man having had a child so late in life. But I . . . I thought Mattey would be beside my deathbed. How could I have even considered that I would stand beside his.

Mattey was so full of life. He lived it every day, brightly and joyously. He was kind, generous, and the most loving child I had ever seen. I know, I know, what else would a mother say? If you could only but hear his laughter! All that knew him loved him, but of course none more than me. He was my very life. It goes against nature for a mother to outlive her child. This is why I still walk these streets.

While I lived, I sought a way for Mattey's name to live on. I thought of our time together, the joy of seeing him learn, and it came to me. I would open a school in Mattey's name. Not for those with advantage, but a school for the poor. Mattey would have wanted it thus. So a school it was to be. A school in my child's name. Mattey's school for the poor.

For a time, I was at peace. Soon it became harder to see, harder to rise, harder to conduct my daily routines.

The only family I had to care for me in my advanced age were in England. It broke my heart that I could not live out my days observing the school, hearing the laughter of the children, and watching always over Mattey and James's tomb. But I had no other choice.

I left ample funds. I left with the promise that the school would flourish, and I said my good-byes to Mattey and James there in the graveyard. I made my way to Middlesex, England. There in Bedfont Parish, you will find a stone that reads:

Here lieth the Body
Of Mary Whaley
Granddaughter to
Francis Page,
of Hatton, and Widdow of James Whaley,
Gentlemen in ye County
of York and ye Colony of
Virginia.
She died ye 31 of Janr
1742.

When my spirit left this earth, I searched for Mattey, but I could not find him. I was tormented by the fear that he was suffering. My spirit flew to this place, to his tomb, but all was as it should be. And then I heard his laughter, and I knew that he was still here, playing joyfully along these streets. I learned also that my school, Mattey's school, was no longer serving the children of the poor, and I grew angry.

It was clear what I had wanted, and there were funds set aside, yet the men that I trusted would not honor my last wishes. This was more than I could bear, but I could do nothing, for I had no voice to speak or body to act. Mattey's name was uttered no more in joy but in bitterness and contention over matters of finance.

Then fate, the same winds of fate that dealt me the horrible blow of taking my child, turned in my favor. The College of William and Mary interceded and settled the matter. The funds were used to build the Grammar and Mattey Practice and Model School. Though it did not serve children, it provided for those that would teach them. Then a wondrous benefactor stepped in, and my dream became reality once again.

Finally, I am at peace, for it has been accomplished what I first intended to do. If you travel north and take the small path near the Governor's Palace, you will find the Matthew Whaley Elementary School. It serves all children, rich and poor, there are no masters and no servants, all are free to learn, all are joyous and carefree, and there are many, many children. And Mattey's name once again lives in the city of Williamsburg.

For Mattey, it is the same now in death as it was in life. He plays carefree and joyous, not ready, as he never was, for his rest. So I linger, and I watch over as a mother would, and I wait for the time when Mattey will seek his eternal rest. So if you feel a wisp of the wind blow about you, or you hear laughter in the breeze, you will know that it is Mattey playing still.

PARADISE LOST

SHARON ROGERS

HAVE YOU COME TO HELP ME? I have been waiting for someone. I have been locked out of my house and cannot find the key. I live down the way . . . there, you can see it. The two-story brick house. It is a grand house, built by my father when I was a girl. Well, I've lived in it now only since coming back to Virginia from Europe after my husband died. But, I do not understand why I am locked out. I did not lock it. I do not know who would wish to keep me out. It is my house!

Someone must be doing this to me on purpose, to torture me, to drive me mad. What if I am dead and cursed to be here for all time? Am I not even to have the comfort of the one place I long for the most, my own home? Or perhaps I am quite confused over the whole matter. Allow me to pause for just a moment and gather my thoughts for they seem to have scattered to the four winds.

Maybe I am utterly and completely mad! So what if I am! You have heard, I suppose, of the eccentric Lucy

Ludwell Paradise? Well, I am she. I am the one about whom they gossiped, whom they maligned. Hypocrites they all were, for it is hypocrisy to befriend someone to their face and then use them as fodder for ridicule! That is how they all were; none were true. All of my husband's friends in London pitied him for being saddled with one such as I. They pitied him?! Had they forgotten who I am! I am a Ludwell of Virginia! With social position and a tobacco fortune. The Ludwell men counseled governors, administered parishes, and governed the colony of Virginia for three generations.

My husband's friends said that I was a tiresome silly woman who only talked of her family. Who did they think they were? My family was more important than the scholarly pursuits that they rambled on about. Things my husband said I would never understand.

Did they think that I would not hear, that I would not be hurt? Well, I never did let them see the pain they caused. Instead I showed anger and rage. At one of our dinners, one of them made a remark that offended me. I took the silver tea urn sitting beside me, walked to him, and poured the boiling contents upon his head and shoulders. I enjoyed it immensely.

But what did any of them matter to me. They were just people passing by. It was my own family turning against me that hurt the most. John, my husband, who doted on me in the beginning, grew weak, spineless, and fearful of everything, even the weather. Every time it stormed, he would hide from the thunder. So to keep control in my household, I thundered as often as I could.

The greatest storm arose over the matter of my elder daughter's marriage. John said that I had lost my mind introducing her to society before her fourteenth year, but

I had plans, dreams. She would have a title and the respect they had never given me. An Italian count became interested. John said that he only sought a fortune that was not there. Against his wishes, I helped them elope. But it was just as John thought. When the count discovered there was no fortune, he took her away from us and forbid us to see her or their children ever again.

John and I could not live together for a time after that. He stayed in Paris, I in London, until an opportunity came to travel here to the colonies—the place of my youth. We reconciled, and it was glorious. We traveled to Philadelphia, New York, Mount Vernon. It was there that we received the news. You see, our younger daughter had been in boarding school, and we received word that she had died. Of course we returned to London immediately. John grew even more fearful and never left London again. He died some time after. I lived there ten more years before I finally returned to Williamsburg, to the house my father built.

My nieces had inherited the house from my sister and her husband, and they allowed me residence. The people here treated me the same as in England! They conspired against me! Said that I had grown erratic, odd, and unpredictable. They decided that I should be in the hospital down the road, the hospital for the deranged. Oh, they would come to visit. But it was just to stare, just to gossip. They never knew what happened there when they left, of the long nights in the dark with the screams all around me, of the treatments for illnesses I didn't even know I had.

I would do the one thing I could. I would think. I would think of all those people who had maligned me, those in London, those in Williamsburg, my own daughters for deserting me, and my husband, and I cursed them all. But more than that I cursed God for allowing it all to happen, and it is for that reason that I know that I am cursed to be here for all time without the comfort of the one place I yearn for the most, my own home.

There are times, though, when I find the house unlocked, and I always enter and I always make my presence known, a footstep here or there, water running when it shouldn't, for I do not want them to forget that that house is the house of Lucy Ludwell Paradise.

Well, I will be on my way to see if perhaps the door is unlocked again, but I will leave you with one last thought. As you go about these streets and spy those who are dressed such as I, ask yourselves, are they of your world or the next? You of short sight would be amazed to know that there are always ghosts amongst you.

SOURCES

Most of the stories in this book were derived from evening programs of the Colonial Williamsburg Foundation, including "Cry Witch" and "Ghosts Amongst Us." Some of these stories are told here in much the same form as they have been told in the programs. Others have not been told in the programs but are derived from research done for those programs.

We Are All Around You

According to a report in the November 24, 1738, *Virginia Gazette,* a man named Anthony Francis Dittond was hung for murder in Williamsburg, and the rope did break on him. He died when he was hung the second time. Another story that can be tied to that account is told in this book as "The Hanging."

The Palace Nurse

On December 22, 1781, a fire that may have begun in the basement of the Governor's Palace destroyed the building. A Philadelphia newspaper account said:

> Saturday night the 22d . . . the palace in the city of Williamsburg, which is supposed to have been set on fire by some malicious person, was in three hours burnt to the ground. This elegant building was for some time past used as an hospital, and upwards of an hundred sick and wounded soldiers were in it when the fire was discovered, but by the timely exertions of a few people, only one perished in the flames.

In addition to the soldiers who died during the Revolutionary War, ten- to eighteen-year-old boys who played the fifes and drums also lost their lives. Fifers and drummers were an important part of the military—both American and European—in the eighteenth century. Their job was to communicate simple orders to the troops and sometimes to communicate with the enemy. Although they did not go into combat, they were still in danger from enemy fire, disease, starvation, and the elements.

Sawney Bean

It is not at all clear what fact, if any, the gruesome legend of Alexander Sawney Bean is based on. The story goes back at least to early eighteenth-century Scotland when it was printed in broadsides or chapbooks, four-page inexpensive booklets sold at fairs, by itinerant peddlers, and at executions. As the eighteenth century progressed, the Sawney Bean story along with other crime stories were gathered into larger publications, which sold as popular reading and also to dissuade young and old alike from a life of crime.

Remember Me

American soldiers endured numerous hardships during the war, brought on by a new country ill-equipped to deal with unforeseen challenges, such as pay shortages, inadequate clothing, scarce food rations, insufficient military arms, and the lack of medical staff and equipment. About 25,000 Americans died in the Revolutionary War, about 6,800 in battle and over 18,000 from disease or exposure, thousands of whom were in British prisons.

The man in the story might well represent any of hundreds of Virginian soldiers who fought for General Washington throughout the colonies and ended up back in Virginia fighting at the Battle of Yorktown in the fall of 1781. Many of the wounded were transported to the Governor's Palace for medical attention. The Palace served as a hospital earlier in the war as well. Some 156 soldiers from the battle and two women are buried in the Palace garden.

The Witch of Pungo

Though we do not know if this case was ever actually heard in the General Court at Williamsburg, we do know that Grace Sherwood was a real person and that she was prosecuted for witchcraft at the county court of Princess Anne County. Authorities in Princess Anne County ordered she be "ducked" in water: if she sank, she would be declared innocent, and if she floated she would be declared a witch. The ducking took place in the Lynnhaven River off what is today known as Witchduck Point. After being thrown from a boat, Sherwood managed to untie herself and rise to the surface, thus proving her guilt.

The Virginia Historical Society has in its collection an early nineteenth-century copy of the following July 1706 Princess Anne County records pertaining to the Sherwood trial:

> Whereas on complaint of Luke Hill in behalf of her Magesty that now is ag[ains]t: Grace Sherrwood for a person suspected of witchcraft & having had sundry evidences sworne agt: her proving many cercumstances & which she could not make any excuse or little or nothing to say in her own behalf [,] only seemed to rely on w[ha]t. the Court should doe & thereupon consented to be tryed in the water & likewise to be serched againe with experim[en]ts being tryed & she swimming[.] W[he]n therein & bound contrary to custom & the Judg[men]ts. of all the spectators & afterwards being serched by five antient weamen who have all declared on oath that she is not

like them nor noe other women that they knew of having two things like titts on her private parts of a Black coller [color] being blacker than the rest of her body all which cercumstance the Court weighing in their consideration doe therefore ord[e]r. that the Sherr: take the s[ai]d. Grace into his custody & comit her body to the common Jaol of this County [Princess Anne County jail] their to secure her by irons or otherwise there to remain till such time as he shall be otherwise directed in ord[e]r. for her coming to the common gaol of the Country [public gaol in Williamsburg] to be brought to a future tryall there [in the General Court].

Hitchhiking Spirit

A version of this story is included in *Shuckin' and Jivin': Folklore from Contemporary Black Americans,* ed. Daryl Cumber Dance (Bloomington: Indiana University Press, 1978), 33.

Broken Heart

A descendant of the Mordecai Cooke family of Glouces-ter, Virginia, told a version of this story to Pete Wrike, a lo-cal historian who was teaching a class called "Ghosts, Leg-ends, and Strange Stories" at Rappahannock Community College.

Dark Corners

Moses Riggs was a jobber (handyman) who murdered a young Negro slave by the name of Stepney in the county of Accomack in 1770. An account of the murder with many of the same details in this story can be found in Accomack County records. One witness at the trial testified that Riggs "said that he had killed the Devil." Another said that he "had the Barrel of a Gun in his hand which was Bloody and had brains upon it" (Accomack County Court Order,

November 1770, Reel 85 at Library of Virginia, 116–119). Other colonial records indicate that Riggs was sentenced to death, appeared to be insane, and was recommended as a "fit Object of Mercy" *(Executive Journals of the Council of Colonial Virginia,* vol. 6, ed. Benjamin J. Hillman [Richmond: Virginia State Library, 1966], 383) and that in May 1776 it was "ordered that Moses Riggs be discharged from his Confinement in the publick Gaol" (Minutes of the Fifth Virginia Convention, in *Revolutionary Virginia: A Documentary Record,* vol. 7, pt. 2, comp. and ed. Brent Tartar [Charlottesville: University Press of Virginia, 1983]). The belief that demons congregate in corners, specifically corners at right angles, is an ancient one in many cultures.

Turning Skull

Based on the following report in the July 27, 1739, *Virginia Gazette* (published by William Parks):

> *From the Paris A la-main, May 24*
> They write from Macon, near Cogent upon the River Seine, that two men digging a Grave in a Church yard there, found a Skull, which they laid upon the Grass by them; but soon after, perceiving it stirring, they ran to the Curé (Parson) and told him there was a Saint buried in the Place where they had been digging. The Curé immediately posted thither, and to his great Surprize found the Skull moving, upon which he cry'd out, a Miracle! a Miracle! as did likewise those that came with him; but not being willing to leave so precious a Relick behind him, he sent for a Cross and Holy Water, his Surplice, Stole and Cap, order'd all the Bells to be rung, and sent notice to the Parishioners, who immediately throng'd to the Place: Then he caus'd a Dish to be brought, put the Skull into it, covered it with a Napkin, and carry'd it into the Church, in Procession, during which, great Debates arose among his Parishioners, every one of them insisting

that Somebody or another of their Family had been buried there. The Curé being arriv'd in the Church, the Skull was laid on the High-Altar, and he began to sing *Te Deum;* but when they came to the Verse *Te per orbem Terrarum,* a Mole starting out of the Skull, discover'd the Cause of its Motion; upon which the Curé broke off *Te Deum,* and the Congregation dispers'd.

The Telltale Finger

This story was one of many ghost stories collected between 1937 and 1942 by Richard Chase of the Virginia Writers' Project, which was administered by the federal government's Works Project Administration (WPA) during the Depression. Chase's text, which is included in the WPA records in the Virginia State Library and Archives, was reprinted in the summer 1993 issue of *Virginia Cavalcade.*

Black Ink

Based on the following report in the October 15, 1767, *Virginia Gazette* (published by Alexander Purdie and John Dixon):

On Friday evening, the 23d of July, there happened a very great storm at Paris, which was succeeded by thunder and lightening for nearly two hours, and gave birth to the following whimsical circumstance. About midnight a certain Gentleman of fortune, newly married, and a bigot, being suddenly awakened by his spouse, was so terrified that he immediately jumped out of bed, and knowing there was a bottle of holy water in a closet in his room, he went to take it out, without any more light than that of the constant lightning, and soon began to sprinkle his Lady, himself, and even the very furniture, to engage, without doubt the protection of Providence. The bottle being quite out, and the storm abating a little, he returned to bed pretty well composed, and began to value himself highly on the efficacy of his operation; but how great his surprise when at daylight he awoke and turned towards his Lady, who he found as black as a curl-pated inhabitant of Africa, and all the bedding, tapestry, and furniture of the room, of the same melancholy complexion. Greatly at a loss what to think, he at first imagined that it was the effect of the lightning, but one of the servants coming in, acquainted him that instead of taking the bottle of holy water he had snatched up the bottle of ink, which stood in the same closet, and emptied it in the place of the consecrated element. Enraged at his mistake, which will cost him a good many loius d'ors, as his furniture was entirely new, he was cured of his superstition, and swore he would have nothing to do with the tricks of the church, as they might possibly lead him some time or another into fresh errours and distress.

Gentleman Robber

Based on the following report in the February 24, 1774, *Virginia Gazette* (published by Alexander Purdie and John Dixon):

> Robberies are now committed by two or three very genteel Highwaymen in different parts of Essex. A few Days ago a Gentleman was accosted in this Manner by one of these polite Highwaymen. Sir, do you see that Gentleman that rides before you? Yes, Sir, says the other; what then? Why, says he that asked the Question, he is a Robber; look behind you, and observe that Man that follows us, he will certainly rob you as he has me. What shall I do? replied the other. Why deliver to me your money, and you will be safe; for as he knows I am robbed, he will not suspect me. Upon this the Gentleman gave his Purse to this officious Gentleman, who rode on pretty smartly before him. Soon after, the highwayman got up to the gentleman who parted with his Money, and asked him if he spoke with that Man that rode on a little before? Yes Sir,

said the Gentleman. O then, replied the other, you are very safe; I give you my Word none of my Friends will meddle with you, for he is one of us.

Selling Teeth

Based on the following report in the November 5, 1767, *Virginia Gazette* (published by Alexander Purdie and John Dixon):

> *August* 8. Monday last an odd accident happened. A master chimneysweeper, who lives in Burleigh Street, having several apprentice boys, was employed to sweep the chimnies of a Lady's house at the Court end of the town. The Lady had the curiosity to stand by, and observing one of the boys to have a fine white set of teeth, asked if he would sell any of them. The poor child willingly consented, and the master asked three guineas for a couple, to pick and choose where she pleased. The bargain was struck, a tooth drawer sent for, who instantly whipped out a couple, the money was paid, and away went Jack and his master well contented; but before they got home the master stopped to buy Jack a pair of silver buckles, with which the poor child was satisfied for his share, and went home and ordered a gallon of beer to regale his family, changed another of the guineas, and received a crooked quarter guinea in part, which putting in his mouth whilst he reckoned the rest of the change, it slipped in his throat, where it now remains, and he is in St. George's hospital, past all hopes of recovery, notwithstanding the efforts of the eminent surgeons of that place.

The Little Shepherd

Based on the following report in the April 23, 1772, *Virginia Gazette* (published by Alexander Purdie and John Dixon):

LONDON:

January 11. On Monday last, about ten o'Clock in the Forenoon, a most surprising Affair happened at the House of Mrs. Golding at Stockwell. All the China, Glasses, Stone Ware, Pewter, Brasses, and other Furniture, began to fall down from their Places, and break to Pieces. This continued slowly for some Time, till the Lady could no longer stay in her House; but went next Door to Mr. Gresham's, where she lost her senses. Her Niece being sent for, had her blooded; and as soon as the Blood was cold in the Bason [basin] it flew out on the Floor, and presently the Bason broke to Pieces. She was obliged to remove from Mr. Gresham's, as the same Damages began in his House; her maid was with her the whole Time. She then went to her Niece (Mrs. Payne) a Farmer in Brixton County, where almost every Thing was destroyed in the House by the same invisible Agent; her Maid was still with her, who seemed quite unconcerned the whole Time. She then went over the Way to Mr. Fowler, at the Brick Pond, where the same Scene followed her, and was obliged to return to her own House, when the few Things which were left began to move and break. They sent the Maid away on an Errand, to try what Effect that would have, when every Thing immediately ceased; upon which, when she returned, they discharged her, and all has continued quiet ever since. The old Lady, it is thought, cannot recover. The above are absolute Facts, though not the Hundreth Part of what happened; the Whole of which is preparing to be laid before the candid and impartial Publick, properly attested and authenticated. One Circumstance, as it is the most remarkable, should not be omitted: some Plates of Mr. Gresham's by the Way of Trial, were placed upon the same shelf with those of Mrs. Golding; the former stood unhurt, but the Whole of Mrs. Golding's were broke in Pieces.

The Ghostly Drummer Boy

Stories of a ghostly drummer made regular appearances in the south of England during the seventeenth century. In the October 1950 issue of the *William and Mary Quarterly* (vol. 7, no. 4), Alfred Owen Aldridge traced the story's migration to Pennsylvania. Our knowledge of the drummer of Pennsylvania comes from an anonymous letter that appeared in Benjamin Franklin's *Pennsylvania Gazette* of April 16–23, 1730. The writer, after describing his own skeptical proclivities, explained how hearing the story from his reverend friend changed him: "I who used to sleep without drawing my Curtains, am now so fearful, that I pin them every Night I go to Bed with corking pins, and cover my self Head over Ears with the Clothes." Aldridge suspected that the letter may have been written by Franklin as part of a campaign against religious superstition.

Dead Man's Grip

A version of this story is included in *Shuckin' and Jivin': Folklore from Contemporary Black Americans,* ed. Daryl Cumber Dance (Bloomington: Indiana University Press, 1978), 27. Other cultures also have versions of this story.

Blackbeard's Courtship

A version of this story is told by Catherine Albertson in *In Ancient Albemarle* (Raleigh: North Carolina Society Daughters of the Revolution, 1914), 57–60. Albertson noted that the town of Bath, North Carolina, where Blackbeard stayed for a month or so, is the source and setting of many tales about the pirate.

Where the Ghost Dog Ran

This is a traditional Cherokee legend. A version can be

found in James Mooney's *Myths of the Cherokees,* originally published in 1900 and republished in *James Mooney's History, Myths, and Sacred Formulas of the Cherokees* (Asheville, NC: Historical Images, 1992), 259.

The Houseguest

The following report on vampires appeared in the March 1732 issue of *The Gentleman's Magazine* of London (*The Gentleman's Magazine, or, Monthly Intelligencer,* vol. 2, 681):

> From *Medreyga in Hungary,* That certain dead Bodies called *Vampyres,* had kill'd several Persons by sucking out all their Blood. The Commander in Chief, and Magistrates of the Place were severally examin'd and unanimously declared, that about 5 years ago, a certain Heyduke named *Arnold Paul,* in his Life Time was heard to say, he had been tormented by a *Vampyre,* and that for a Remedy he had eaten some of the Earth of the *Vampyre's* Graves, and rubbed himself with their Blood. That 20 or 30 Days after the Death of the said *Arnold Paul,* several Persons complained they were tormented; and that he had taken away the Lives of 4 Persons. To put a Stop to such a Calamity, the Inhabitants [. . .] took up his Body, 40 Days after he had been dead and found it fresh and free from Corruption; that he bled at the Nose, Mouth and Ears, pure and florid Blood; that his Shroud and Winding Sheet were all over Bloody; and that his Finger and Toe Nails were fallen off, and new ones grown in their room. By these circumstances they were persuaded he was a *Vampyre,* and, according to Custom, drove a stake thro' his heart; at which he gave a horrid Groan. They burnt his Body to Ashes, and threw them into his Grave. 'Twas added, that those who have been tormented, or killed by the *Vampyres* become *Vampyres* when they are dead. Upon which Account they served several other dead bodies as they had done *Arnold Paul's,* for tormenting the living.

The Gamble

A version of this story is told in *Virginia Supernatural Tales* by George Holbert Tucker (Norfolk, VA: Donning Company, 1977), 40–42.

The Cheater

Based on the following report in the July 11, 1766, *Virginia Gazette* (published by Alexander Purdie and John Dixon):

> Gloucester, March 17. We have an account of a very extraordinary instance of the divine vengeance that happened about a week ago at Chalford in this county. One Richard Parsons, a young man of that place, was playing at cards, and he most profanely wished his flesh might rot, and his eyes never shut, if he did not win the next game. When he was going to bed, he observed a black spot upon his leg, from which a mortification began immediately to spread all over his body, so that he died in a day or two, his flesh being quite rotten; nor would his eyes be shut, notwithstanding all the efforts of his friends to close them. The truth of this fact is attested by many of the neighbours who were with him.

In the Rigging

Based on the following report in the December 23, 1775, *Virginia Gazette* (published by Alexander Purdie and John Dixon):

> London, Sept. 1,
> Last week a beautiful young girl, about 18 years of age, in boy's clothes, shipped herself on board a vessel in the river bound to the West Indies; but her sex being accidentally discovered, prevented her from her intended voyage. She had passed for a boy some time, and had

lived near a twelvemonth as a footman to a Lady, and said her desire of seeing the world occasioned her to disguise her sex, and choose a sailor's life.

Perils of Conscience

The February 25, 1737, *Virginia Gazette* (published by William Parks) included the following report:

> *Ran away, last* January, *from* Charles Chiswell, *Esq; of* Hanover *County, a Servant Man, nam'd* William Marr, *an* Irishman, *aged about* 30, *of a middle Stature, and a brown Complexion. He wore a Kersey Coat, with Mettal Buttons. He cross'd over* Potomack, *on the Ice, below* Ockoquan, *and hath been seen* in Maryland.
>
> *Whoever will secure the said Servant, so that his Master may have him again, shall have Twenty shillings Reward, besides what the Law allows.*
>
> Charles Chiswell.

That was followed, in the June 10, 1737, *Gazette* (also published by Parks) with this report:

> We hear also, from *Hanover* County, That one William Marr, a servant of Col. *John Chiswell's,* came from his said Master's, to the Courthouse on Saturday last, and inform'd the King's Deputy-Attorney, that he was concern'd in the Murder of a Man; upon which he took him before *Robert Lewis,* and *Richard Clough,* Gent. Two of his Majesty's Justices of that County, where he voluntarily confess'd as follows: That he ran away some Time ago, and joyn'd in Company with 3 other Servants, viz. Peter Heckie, Matthew O Conner, and Bryan Conner, belonging to Capt. Avery, and his Son, of *Prince William* County, who were also ran away from their Masters; that he the said Marr, and the 3 other Servants, went far back in the Woods, and on the last Day of April, they came to a Cabbin near Great Cape Capon-Creek, in *Orange*

County, in which was one Liselet Larby, (a Person who liv'd by Hunting) and after staying all Night with him, and being entertain'd as well as cou'd be expected in such a Place, the said Liselet Larby having Occasion to go down among the Inhabitants, to buy Powder and Shot, he set out the next Day, and the said 4 Men with him, in seeming Friendship, about 250 Yards, and they suspecting the Said Larby wou'd discover to the Inhabitants where the said Runaways were, one of them propos'd killing him, and it being consented to by the rest, Peter Heckie, the first Proposer, shot the said Liselet Larby thro' the Back with a Gun of the said Liselet's, and afterwards beat his Brains out with the But End thereof, and went away, leaving him in that Condition. That the said Marr being very uneasy in his Mind that he had consented to such a barbarous Murder, and being also apprehensive that the other 3 who were all Ship-Mates, and he a Stranger to them, might kill him too, took the first Opportunity to leave them, and accordingly did; but being taken up in the lower Parts of *Orange* County, was sent from Constable to Constable to his late Master's House. He having a Remorse of Conscience, and being terrify'd (as he says) by the Apparition of the murder'd Man, he cou'd not rest till he discover'd the Murder, and accordingly came to the Court-house this Day, and made his Information and Confession, (which the above is the Substance of) which he sign'd; and was thereupon committed to the Goal of that County, in Order for a further Examination.

He gives a frightful Account of the Apparation of the murder'd Man's tormenting him; which seems incredible, and as if the Man was out of his Senses; but that the Circumstances of his whole Account of the Fact, the Pertinency of his Answers, and his Behaviour in the Examination, shew him to be otherwise. He says, that upon his giving this Account, when he came back to the Inhabitants, Two Men with good Horses went in Pursuit of the said Three Men, who were gone towards *Allegainy,* far back beyond the Mountains, and were in Hopes of taking them.

Dismal Swamp

The history of this tale is traced in *Virginia Supernatural Tales* by George Holbert Tucker (Norfolk, VA: Donning Company, 1977), 50–53. The Dismal Swamp, a marshy area extending south from Virginia across the North Carolina border with Lake Drummond in its center, was already the setting for a ghost story when the Irish poet Thomas Moore visited Virginia in 1803 and 1804. Moore used the story as the basis for a poem, "The Lake of the Dismal Swamp," that was first published in 1806. Moore prefaced his poem as follows:

> They tell of a young man, who lost his mind upon the death of a girl he loved, and who, suddenly disappearing from his friends, was never afterwards heard of. As he had frequently said, in his ravings, that the girl was not dead, but had gone to the Dismal Swamp, it is supposed he had wandered into that dreary wilderness, and had died of hunger, or had been lost in some of its dreadful morasses.

The poem's final stanza reads:

> But oft, from the Indian hunter's camp
> This lover and maid so true
> Are seen at the hour of midnight damp
> To cross the Lake by a fire-fly lamp,
> And paddle their white canoe!

The Combustible Woman

Based on the following report in the June 17, 1737, *Virginia Gazette* (published by William Parks):

Extract of a letter from Verona, *on a surprising Accident, which befel a Woman at* Cerena, *a City of* Romagna.

THIS Woman was 62 Years of Age, and had been used to wash and rub herself every Day with Spirit of Camphire, to prevent Colds, and Coughs. On the 14th of *March* 1731, in the Evening, she went up to her Room without any unusual Symptom, only that she seemed somewhat melancholly. In the Morning she was found near her Bed burnt to Ashes, all but her Shin-bones, and Feet, and Three Fingers of one Hand: The Ashes were clammy, and stunk intolerably. The Walls of the Room, the Bed, and other Furniture, were covered with a fine but moist Dust, which had penetrated into the Chamber above it. The Ceiling was almost covered with a Sort of Moisture of a dark yellow colour, which gave a very offensive Smell. Those Parts of the Body that remain'd, were of a blackish Hue; nothing else in the Room was consum'd, only the Tallow of Two Candles quite melted, but the Wick not burnt: The blackish Hue of the Remains of the Body, the Consumption of the other Parts, and their Reduction to Ashes, were evident Proofs of a Fire: Yet common Fire can hardly reduce so large a Body to Ashes; for it has often appear'd, that in great Conflagrations, the Bodies have been dried, scorched, and somewhat burnt in the external Parts, but not entirely consum'd. 'Tis likewise certain, that common Fire would have taken hold of the Beds, the Chamber, and even the whole House: Besides, there was neither Fire nor Light in the Chamber, and the Serenity of the Air left no Room to suspect, that there was any Lightning that could produce such an Accident; because there was not the least Hole found in the Sides of the Chamber. 'Tis therefore not unreasonable to conclude, that this poor Woman was consum'd by a Fire that kindled within her own Body, proceeding from the oily Particles of the mentioned Spirits, excited by chafing, and the Heat of her Constitution. These are the Thoughts of Signoir *Muffei,* and Father *Bellivaga,* which are corroborated by the Examples of Powder Magazines, for the

Exhalations from the Powder, being put into a violent
Motion by some external Cause, have sometimes blown
up the Magazine without the Help of any apparent Fire.
A human Body hath likewise in it some oleous and sa-
line Particles, capable of producing a Fire: We even find,
that the Sweat of some People, smells like Brimstone.
Phesphoruses are made of Urine, which partly kindle of
themselves: Therefore, if to these Particles of the Body,
Brandy and Camphire be added, the Two Ingredients
which compose the Spirit of Camphire, their Particles
especially, by the Means of chafing, cannot but cause a violent Motion in the mention'd Particles of the Blood, and
other Juices, which will produce a vehement Attrition,
or rubbing against each other: Such Attrition is capable
of producing Fire even in cold Bodies, as appears by the
striking of a Piece of Steel upon a Flint, and the rubbing
of Two Sticks against each other: The Sun draws every
Day from Bodies, not the most combustible, Vapours,
which produce Fire, when put up in a narrow Compass.
If we cause a Quantity of Camphire to evaporate in a
close Chamber till it is fill'd with the Vapour, and then
enter it with a lighted Torch, the Vapour takes Fire at
once, and causes a Flash like that of Lightning: Besides
all this, the Fermentation of the Juices in the Woman's
Body, may have contributed something to the Effect; for
a Flame is often produced by the Mixture and Fermentation of certain Liquors. The Reason why the Shin-bones
and the Feet were not burnt, may be this, that she did not
chafe those Parts with the mention'd Spirits, or at least
not so much as the other Parts of the Body; and possibly,
she never used the Three Fingers that remain'd uncon-
sum'd, in chafing: The Oiliness of the Ashes, 'tis likely,
proceeded from the Fat of the Body: As the Fire was kindled at once in the Veins, and most minute Vessels of the
Body, we may conclude, that it consum'd it in a Moment;
which sudden Effect could not have been produced by
other Fires, that were not so inclosed in the Body. Some
Effect of this Fire was found in the upper Rooms, because

such a sudden Heat flies chiefly upward; which was likewise the Cause that the Floor of her Chamber escaped being burnt, and that none of the Furniture was touch'd: For a Piece of Paper may be drawn suddenly through the greatest Flame without being set on Fire.

Marriage Plans

A version of this story is told in Joseph Jacobs's *English Fairy Tales* (New York, NY: Everyman's Library, 1993), originally published in 1890.

Drowning in Fashion

Based on the following report in the June 11, 1767, *Virginia Gazette* (published by Alexander Purdie and John Dixon):

> A few days ago some Gentlemen going down to Greenwich, on a party of pleasure upon the water with several Ladies, their boat was unfortunately overset by a collier, and they all were in the greatest danger of losing their lives. Among the rest was a Lady, who was seen by her servant to go to the bottom: The fellow, with a most becoming spirit, leaped into the water to save his mistress, and, being a good diver, got hold of his Lady in a very particular manner; he was afraid of her confining his arms, and hindering his swimming, and therefore dexterously caught her by the head of hair in his teeth, and was bringing her very safely and skillfully to shore. But she being in the fashion, that part of hair which he held in his teeth came off, and down the Lady went the second time to the bottom; so that unless the honest diver had been as resolute as skillful, and plunged again after her and saved her, she must have fallen a sacrifice to a French fashion, and too dearly convinced her sex that when they leave off to follow nature they must always go astray, or to the bottom.

Deadly Error

Based on a report in the December 23, 1775, *Virginia Gazette* (published by John Dixon and William Hunter), which was taken from a story in the London *Evening Post*:

From the London Evening-Post.

The following is said to be a true relation of what happened at the burning of Charlestown, in America.—"In the confusion, while part of the town was in flames, a Scotch soldier belonging to the regulars forced his way into one of the houses, where he found in one of the rooms a woman just coming out with her daughter about five years old, in her hand, to go to her husband's chamber, where he was confined by illness, to assist him in his escape. The mother on her knees, and the little infant, who following the example of her mother, begged that the soldier would spare their lives, they conceiving the ruffian intended to murder them. The screams of the mother and daughter reached the room where the husband lay, and though he had been confined for a long time to his bed, he leaped up, and with a drawn sword in his hand, rushed into the apartment which was the scene of distress, and instantly run the soldier through the body. The wretch, though mortally wounded, had just time to turn about to see from whom he had received this condign punishment, when, to his astonishment and confusion, he discovered the injured person to be his brother, and died. The unfortunate husband had but just time to see his wife lying in a fit, his child running about in a phrenzy, his brother lying dead at his feet; and having cried out, "I have killed my brother!" fell down in a swoon. The nurse, who had followed her master, had just heard his last words, when she perceived the house in flame, and running forth, in hopes to get assistance to save this unfortunate family, had just got out of the house, when the roof, which had first taken fire, fell. It was some days before the nurse recovered her recollection, sufficient to give any account of this fatal event, but it now appears that the unfortunate husband had left Scotland about seven years ago, and gone to settle in New England, where he shortly after married much to his advantage, and soon afterwards went to settle at Charlestown, where he lived with great credit and in domestic happiness till the day of that general confusion.

The Abiku

A version of this story titled "Susanna and Simon" originally appeared in Joel Chandler Harris's book *Daddy Jake, the Runaway, and Short Stories Told after Dark* (Freeport, NY: Books for Libraries Press, 1972), originally published in 1889. Harris noted that this story was told to one of his children by an African American storyteller named John Holder and that he had found variants (or perhaps the original) among Bantu-speaking tribes.

The Hanging

The following report appeared in the August 25, 1738, *Virginia Gazette* (published by William Parks):

> Last *Tuesday, Anthony-Francis Dittond,* was brought from Spotsylvania County, and committed to the Public Goal in this City, being charged with barbarously murdering Mr. *Evans,* Coachmaker, mentioned in our last; the wearing Apparel, Horse, Bridle, Saddle, and Portmanteau, etc., of the Deceased, being found upon him.

That was followed by this report in the November 24, 1738, *Virginia Gazette:*

> This Day *Anthony Francis Dittond,* who receiv'd Sentence

of Death, at the last General Court, for the Murder of Mr. *Evans,* the Coachmaker, as formerly mentioned, was executed at the usual Place near this City. He was a lusty Man, and after he had been turn'd off about 2 or 3 Minutes, the Executioner bore him down to strangle him and put him out of his Pain the sooner; in doing which, the Rope broke, and the Man fell down senseless and motionless; but in a short space of Time, he recovered his Senses, sate up, and talk'd again, begging the Minister and the Spectators heartily to pray for him. Then got into the Cart again himself, and was hanged till he was dead. His Corps was put into a Coffin; and we hear it is to be annatomiz'd by the Surgeons. Whilst he was in Prison, he confess'd the Murder.

Icy Hell

A version of this story is told in *The Whale and His Captors* by Henry Cheever (New York, NY: Harper and Brothers, 1853). Cheever sets the story in August 1775. He notes that, "If this strange tale be true, we see that Coleridge's wonderful *Rime of the Ancient Mariner* may not be all fancy, but may have a substantial basis of fact."

Loving Sisters

Sir Peyton Skipwith married Anne Miller and then her sister Jean. The facts, however, end there. Research reveals no evidence of an altercation between the sisters or an affair between Peyton and Jean. Anne died in childbirth, not in the stairway of the Wythe house. It was not until nine years after Anne's death that Peyton and Jean were married, and Jean didn't die until she was seventy-eight years old, well after her husband. Lady Jean Skipwith was one of the most educated women in Virginia and amassed a library of over eight hundred books.

A Mother's Love

After Matthew died, Mary Whaley established the Mattey Free School for the poor on Capitol Landing Road in Williamsburg. It had a schoolhouse, a master's house, and a stable. When Mary Whaley left for England, she entrusted the school's management to the Bruton Parish Church wardens. She died in 1742, leaving a legacy of five hundred British pounds to support the school, but an executor refused to pay, resulting in a suit that dragged on past the Revolution. In 1859, an English lawyer called the church's attention to the still-pending suit. In 1865, the College of William and Mary agreed to discharge the trust of the will and used the legacy to build the Grammar and Mattey Practice and Model School on the then-vacant Governor's Palace grounds. When Colonial Williamsburg acquired and tore down the property in the 1920s to rebuild the Governor's Palace, John D. Rockefeller Jr. replaced it with the Matthew Whaley Elementary School a couple of blocks away. The public school is still in operation today.

Paradise Lost

Philip Ludwell II was one of the richest and most prominent men in the Virginia Colony in the first quarter of the eighteenth century. Among other properties, he owned the Ludwell Tenement, which he willed to his son, Philip Ludwell III. Philip III made improvements to the tenement and also built the two-story brick townhouse now called the Ludwell-Paradise House around 1755. He left the townhouse to his eldest daughter, Hannah Ludwell Lee, and the tenement to his daughter Lucy. Portia Lee Hodgson, Hannah's daughter, inherited the townhouse from her parents and rented it to her widowed aunt, Lucy, when she returned from England in 1805. Lucy gained a reputation for eccentricity and in 1812 was committed to the Public Hospital, an institution for people with mental health disorders.

ABOUT THE CONTRIBUTORS

Roy Bauschatz was a storyteller for Colonial Williamsburg's evening programs.

Melanie Collins worked in Colonial Williamsburg's evening programs and as an actor/interpreter for the Foundation.

Jan Couperthwaite is a historical researcher, actor, and writer. She has performed as a storyteller at Colonial Williamsburg's Fourth of July celebration and at the Colonial Williamsburg Storytelling Festival.

Jonathan Hallman is a cooper for the Colonial Williamsburg Foundation as well as a storyteller and a program manager for evening programs.

John R. Hamant has worked for the Colonial Williamsburg Foundation as an archaeologist, a character interpreter, director of special events and protocol officer, and director of evening and special programs. He helps train storytellers and continues to be a storyteller himself.

John P. Hunter wrote Colonial Williamsburg's *Red Thunder* and *Link to the Past, Bridge to the Future.*

Gaynelle McNichols was the supervisor of the Capitol and Public Gaol in Colonial Williamsburg's Historic Area. Several of the stories about criminals in the Foundation's evening programs are the result of her research about prisoners in the gaol.

Gene Mitchell is the supervisor of the Thomas Everard House and Wetherburn's Tavern in Colonial Williamsburg's Historic Area.

Sharon Rogers was an administrative assistant in Colonial Williamsburg's Media Relations as well as a storyteller and performer in evening programs.

Andrea Squires is a storyteller and writer for Colonial Williamsburg and has been a trainer and theatrical interpreter.

Ruth Tschan was a historical interpreter and storyteller in Colonial Williamsburg's evening programs.

Patti Vaticano was the supervisor of the James Geddy House in Colonial Williamsburg's Historic Area.

Jason Whitehead is the supervisor of Colonial Williamsburg's Masonry Trades/Brickyard.

Donna Wolf has been with Colonial Williamsburg in various capacities, including actor/interpreter, evening programs performer, and master storyteller. She is also a puppeteer and street character performer.

ACKNOWLEDGMENTS

The editors are grateful for the assistance of the following: Janice Bomar, Merritt Capossela, Karen Clancy, Dave Doody, Kathaleen Getward, Erik Goldstein, John Hamant, Thomas Hay, Cathy Hellier, Suzanne Hood, Lindsay Keiter, Marianne Martin, Todd Norris, Susan Pryor, Paul Rider, Linda Rowe, and Peter Wrike.